MIRACLE ON MAPLE STREET

People Are Talking ...

Linda Wood Rondeau does not write your run of the mill romance.

—**Lynn Woods Rix**, *author*

I have really enjoyed Linda Wood Rondeau's style of prose in each of her books thus far and am anticipating her next release.

—**Cathie Werley**, *reader*

I love how Linda Wood Rondeau's stories flow so smoothly and that her characters are believable.

—**JoAnn Stewart**, *reader*

Reading Linda Wood Rondeau's books is like wrapping yourself in your favorite blanket and going on a journey that is much anticipated.

—**Maria Boyea Bourgeois**, *reader*

For a satisfying read, Linda Wood Rondeau delivers original plots, complex characters, and real-life situations that mirror her years as a social worker.

—**Cleo Lampos**, *author, Dust Between the Stiches*

Linda Wood Rondeau's books will grab your heart and not let go.

—**Carol McLain**, *author, The Poison We Drink*

Sparks meets Sue Grafton. The twists and turns keep readers intrigued and soon readers are rooting for the protagonist to succeed against all odds.

—**Gregg Golson**, *reader*

What I love about Linda Wood Rondeau's books: well-developed, ordinary, relatable characters and the sprinkling of humor throughout her books. I love her way with words.

—**Cass Wessel**, *reader*

I am yet to read a book by Linda Wood Rondeau that doesn't contain 3D characters that linger long after the last page is turned.

—**Clare Revell**, *author, Monday's Child series*

Linda Wood Rondeau has a way of putting the reader into the characters' heads. The reader feels invested in the story.

—**Jacqueline Kimball**, *author*

Enjoyable reading. Keeps you guessing. Highly recommended.

—**Toni Palm-Taylor,** *reader*

I am a big fan of Linda Wood Rondeau's books. They always have story lines and wonderful characters that keep me reading.

—**Ann Lacy Ellison**, *reader*

Reviewers Are Saying …

… words that draw you in like the smell of cider on a chilly afternoon. Lovely.

… She keeps you turning pages with her wit, descriptions, humor, and great writing.

… the author has a way with words that is unique and brings to life a story that touches the heart.

… an AMAZING talent & her books NEVER disappoint

… Linda Wood Rondeau is a writer to be watching.

… Her writing style and the way she portrays her characters results in pulling the reader into a story that is hard to put down once you have started it.

… Great warmth and humanity with surprising depth

… this author's writing delivers: suspense, humor and good writing. Books that stick with you!

MIRACLE ON MAPLE STREET

Linda Wood Rondeau

Elk Lake
Publishing, Inc.

Plymouth, Massachusetts

Copyright Notice

Miracle on Maple Street

First edition. Copyright © 2016 by Linda Wood Rondeau. The information contained in this book is the intellectual property of Linda Wood Rondeau and is governed by United States and International copyright laws. All rights reserved. No part of this publication may be reproduced or transmitted in any form or by any means – electronic, mechanical, photocopying, or recording – without express written permission of the publisher. The only exceptions are brief quotations in printed or broadcasted critical articles and reviews.

[BIBLE PERMISSIONS]

Cover and Graphics Design: Jeff Gifford
Interior Design: MelindaMartin.me
Editor: Deb Haggerty

PUBLISHED BY: Elk Lake Publishing, Inc., 35 Dogwood Dr., Plymouth, MA 02360

Library Cataloging Data
Names: Rondeau, Linda Wood (Linda Wood Rondeau)
Title: Miracle on Maple Street / Linda Wood Rondeau
192 p. 23cm × 15cm (9in × 6 in.)
Description: Elk Lake Publishing digital eBook edition | Elk Lake Publishing Trade paperback edition | Massachusetts: Elk Lake Publishing, 2016
Summary: "Christmas is a time for miracles," Ryan McDougal tells his mother, when he is told that a long lost cousin, Millie, has resurfaced after nearly forty years, the cousin whose picture his mother clasped the day his father abandoned him. Though they occurred decades apart, he always believed the two disappearances were connected like opposite links of a chain. With Millie's arrival, perhaps he might finally receive the answers he so desperately sought. However, Ryan has a third thorn in his side, more devastating than any mystery. His wife, the love of his life, has left his arms and his bed. How long before she moves out of the house and takes his beloved son with her? He prays for his own Christmas miracle. Millie's anticipated visit prompts Ryan's mother to reveal secrets that bring all to light. However, when past and present collide, the truth is more than Ryan can bear.
Identifiers: ISBN-13: 978-1-944430-82-5 (POD) | 978-1-944430-83-2 (ebk)
1. Christmas 2. Marriage Problems 3. Family Problems 4. Family Life 5. Past Mistakes 6. Miracles 7. Parents

Dedication

This book is dedicated to all who mourn.

Disappointment is never the end of the road.

God stands ready to turn our pain into purpose.

—Linda Wood Rondeau

Acknowledgments

No manuscript is an author's sole work. To try to thank everyone who has offered good thoughts, prayers, suggestions, and interest would be a book unto itself. But I do want to express my gratitude to all those who gave of their time and efforts, their encouragement when I couldn't see daylight, and for treats along the way.

Thanks once again to Hartline Literary Agency.

Thanks to American Christian Fiction Writers for help with research questions.

A special thank you to Deb Haggerty and the folks at Elk Lake Publishing for the Herculean efforts toward this book and their belief in its message.

A special thank you to Dr. Evelyn Weissman and Dr. Deb Lyon for their time and expertise with medical questions.

Special thanks to my cousin Sharon, the inspiration for this book. Though our paths are very dissimilar to Bertie and Millie's, those memories of our growing up years remain precious.

Thank you to my family and friends who continually offer encouragement and inspiration.

And, of course, a very special thank you to my husband Steve, my mentor and advisor. You have been more than an assistant. You have been my constant encourager, chauffeur, cook, and dishwasher. You have unquestioningly researched my curiosities, though seemingly mundane and unconnected.

Most of all I thank my Lord and Savior for allowing me to continue to write for his glory.

Ryan McDougal
Christmas Eve
1999

Why now? How did I come to this point on *this* night? Willing to throw everything away, like my father did more than twenty years before? Willing to do the very thing for which I'd hated him?

With doomsday predicted by many in the scientific community, the Y2K bug loomed on everyone's mind. What did I care if planes fell from the sky because computers would not accept the year 2000? My world had already collapsed. What more could global chaos do to me?

I'd tried for a year to save my marriage. Didn't tonight prove it was beyond help? Why stay any longer?

Earlier, I finally learned the truth behind the secrets shrouding my life, the trident that pierced my soul. Yet, revelation didn't bring peace. I pulled my jacket collar over my ears as I wandered down Maple Street, my mind jumbled by a lifetime of lies.

Christmas, one more charade to add to the heap. To me, the holiday had become a one-act play where I pretended delight with feigned enthusiasm. For me, the holiday lost its magic many years ago when my father deserted us while I dreamed of transformers under the tree. An eight-year-old doesn't expect to begin his favorite holiday in an upside down world. I woke eager to tear open packages. Instead, I found no presents under the tree, no blueberry muffins, and no turkey in the oven.

My mother sat on a chair. She stared blankly out the kitchen window, a gold-framed photograph on her lap, the picture of the pretty but sullen teenager. For reasons never shared with me, the unnamed girl ran away on her sixteenth birthday. I wondered why, from my earliest memory, her picture held a place of honor on the fireplace mantel.

I shook my mother's shoulder. No response.

Where was my father? He could explain what was wrong—why Christmas dreams turned into yuletide nightmares. I searched for him, first his bedroom then the entire house.

"Mom, where's Pop?"

She clutched the picture to her chest. "He's gone, Ryan."

"Where did he go? It's Christmas. He promised to be here when I woke up."

Pop was a telephone lineman. Whenever he went off for a job, he'd put on his yellow hard hat, rub my head, and say, "Take care of your mother until I get back." If I'd already gone to bed, he'd wake me to give me the order. I always promised I would.

I rushed to the window. There'd been a fresh snowfall overnight. Maybe Pop had been called out. If he hadn't come to wake me, he must have left in an awful hurry. He went someplace to save Christmas for other people. To me, my pop was a superhero in a yellow hard hat.

My gaze wandered to the kitchen table adorned only with my father's yellow hard hat. Superman wouldn't forget his cape. Why did my father leave his hat? My child's heart sensed then I'd never see him again. From that point on, Christmas became another day on the calendar where I nursed a zombie-like woman who preferred her sorrow over her son—a woman who hopelessly waited for her man to come back.

Her energy, what little she possessed, would have been better spent in a job search. Our neighbor helped us get welfare so we wouldn't starve to death. Every Christmas, she brought over a small decorated tree, a ham dinner, and presents. I think there's a special place in heaven for people like Gina Forbes, one of the few true Christians I'd ever known.

Here I was years later, now dealing with the third fork in the trident that pierced my soul. As midnight zeroed in, I took another glance down Maple Street, the place my younger self couldn't wait to leave.

I'd lived with Stone Woman long enough. So two days after high school graduation, I left to begin my Army career. As I walked out the door, my mother lifted her head. Her eyes misted a goodbye. Were the tears for me or my long-lost father? Gina Forbes wrote occasional letters to let me know how Mom fared. I spent my leaves anywhere but home.

After basic training, I served as an MP. Somehow, I missed deployment overseas. A year before my hitch ended, I met Penny, a girl with a voice to match her beauty. We married a week later. When you know you've found the one, there's no need to wait. Nine months later, our boy Ryan Junior came along. To avoid confusion, most everyone called him R.J. I went to his room every night to watch him sleep, and I made the same promise. "I'll never leave you, my sweet sonny boy."

Yet, here I stood. Ready to break the most solemn of promises.

When my Army hitch ended, I wasn't sure what I'd do next. Sometimes life makes those decisions for you. For me, clarity came with a package from Gina Forbes containing a card, a blue quilt for my son, and a handwritten note: *Sorry to tell you that your mother's health has deteriorated. She was in the hospital for a few days last month. The doctor wanted to put her on antidepressants, but she refused to take them. She shouldn't be alone. I've let the doctor know how bad she is. She refuses to go back to the hospital. Yesterday, out of the blue, she asked if I knew where you were. She'd forgotten you'd joined the Army. If you can find it in your heart to forgive your mother for her failures, perhaps you could at least brighten her day with a visit.*

My protests proved moot against Penny's insistence we move into the house on Maple Street to take care of my mother. "Ryan, no matter what your mother did or did not do, she is still the woman who gave you birth."

How was it possible on this night, I stood ready to leave the most wonderful woman in the world?

A grandchild, as well as a daughter-in-law's unconditional love, built the ladder Mom needed to climb out of despair, to the point she went to church with Gina Forbes. Life fell into predictable rhythms of acceptability for all of us on Maple Street. Until last year—when my wife left my bed and moved into the den. For the past year, with each sunrise, I asked myself the same question—*why doesn't my wife love me anymore?*

Nor did the specter of unexplained disappearances ever leave our house. We relegated the unknowns to a corner, like a sulking child. Now my wife's emotional abandonment completed the triangle of mysteries, a geometric spear of perplexity. Even so, we muddled through our existence, actors who performed their monologs on a shared stage.

Funny how life deludes us. One day, reality crashes upon a crafted, albeit imperfect world, which is why I now strolled up and down Maple Street and considered a different existence. Why not join the ranks of those who had disappeared?

For the second time today, I turned to a God I had yet to call my own.

Ryan
Earlier
1999

Mom's smile flashed like a lightning bolt across my imagination. She picked up a stack of breakfast dishes, then smiled again. "Millie's coming."

"Millie who?" I asked.

She tilted her head as if the question were the dumbest she'd ever heard. "My cousin, Millie."

"The girl in the picture?"

Mom nodded. "Only cousin I ever had."

I glanced into the living room where I had a full view of the mantle. A smug satisfaction crept over me. I finally knew her first name. I suppose there was a last name I'd learn later. "Kind of out of the blue, isn't it? I thought you never heard from her after she ran away."

Mom clipped into the living room, grabbed Millie's picture, and put it on the table like a centerpiece. I traced the familiar Christmas tree decorated with popcorn chains. Instinct told me this runaway cousin was somehow connected to my father's disappearance, in spite of the decades between the two events—events Mom refused to talk about. I feared I might go to the grave, my assumptions never confirmed. Anger reared. I pushed it aside. Like an immovable object, my mother's secrets could not be forced into the open.

I gazed at the photograph to study it one more time—although the image had long been seared in my mind. The girl wore a paisley scarf secured by a gold leaf pin. Sunken brown eyes dared me to know her story. Perhaps now, my mother would share what happened to make a young girl leave a family who apparently loved her.

"Was this picture taken before she took off?"

Mom's face drooped. "Yes. The same night."

"Did you ever find out why she ran away?"

My mother never responded to a question she didn't want to answer. Instead, she invented activities as deterrents. She took out a plastic tub from the pantry, her file cabinet for important documents like birth certificates, the property deed, insurance forms, and letters from runaway cousins.

"Mom, you should keep these papers in the fireproof box I bought for you."

She rummaged through the bin's contents. "This works just fine. Why change? Besides, I'm too old to learn new ways."

"Fifty-four's still pretty young, isn't it, Penny?"

My wife didn't answer me, nor did I expect she would. For the past year, except for an occasional *tsk* when I left my coffee cup on the counter, our conversations were limited to reminders about school conferences and doctor appointments. I longed to hold my wife in my arms once again. After she had moved into the den, I worried she'd soon move completely out of my life and take R.J. with her.

"Ryan, leave Penny out of this." Mom lifted out a white envelope as delicately as if it'd been a dried rose petal. "Ah, here it is." She removed the letter from the envelope, then handed it to me. "Millie says she wants to put the past in the past, whatever that means. I don't know how she found me or what her life has been like since she left. I'll be glad to see her no matter what. She says she'll be here later tonight and not to hold supper for her. I could at least make a cake. It's her birthday today."

Mom stopped to take a breath. I looked up at her, amazed. In one paragraph, she'd said more than all of the last week, maybe even the last month. When we first came to live with her, she only talked about R.J. With Penny's encouragement, my mother started to cook again—once her greatest joy before my father left.

"What's for dinner?" I asked.

From the time he learned to talk, my son has selected the Christmas meal. "R.J. wants to have mashed potatoes, corn, Jell-O with whipped cream—the real whipped cream not the store bought kind—and gingerbread cookies for desert."

I usually spent my Christmas Eve afternoons at Belle's Café where my friends challenged me to several games of darts. Since my family would be otherwise occupied, I saw no reason to change my normal agenda except for a nagging curiosity. Nor could I shake the sensation Millie's visit, like the aftermath of a storm, would shake up the life I'd accepted as normal—not a great life but my life.

I glanced at the letter Mom condensed for me. "Will Millie stay over for Christmas?"

My mother had already begun her ritualistic process where she lined up all the ingredients she'd need for the day's cooking marathon. "Don't know if she'll stay tonight. Says she has a room booked in town at Isabel's bed and breakfast."

I could do the math myself, but I wondered if Mom had. "How long since you saw her last?"

"Nearly forty years with no word till this letter. The day she left was the worst day of my life."

How could any day be worse than the day your husband leaves you?

"I'm amazed she found you. Didn't you grow up in Cold Creek?"

Mom nodded while she jabbed the envelope and placed it next to the picture. "I don't know how she found me. I'm glad she did. See, it's addressed to me, Mrs. Bertha McDougal."

I picked up the envelope and glanced at the address. "How did she know your married name?"

"Don't ask me questions I can't answer." Mom yanked the letter from my hand, put it back into the plastic bin, then returned the bin to the pantry. She shut the door with slightly more gusto than required.

Once more I'd pushed my mother into fields of mental exercise she'd resisted since my childhood. "I noticed the return address was Nashville. Wonder how she ended up there?"

"Guess we'll find out soon enough. I don't know if I'll even recognize her when she arrives." Mom wiped down the counter as she shot Penny a woman-to-woman silent message then said, "Oh, well. No need to worry about mysteries that'll be solved before night's end."

Penny rose from the table to help my mother finish gathering ingredients as she read the list from her recipe cards.

"Looks like we're good to start." Mom broke four eggs then whipped the whites in a separate bowl. "So, Ryan, what did you get R.J. for Christmas?"

Although annoyed she'd changed the topic again, I sat up in my chair, full of pride. "Got him his first two-wheeler."

As expected, Penny scowled. *Too bad*. If she'd bother to talk to me, I wouldn't have gone against her wishes. She turned, hands on her hips. "Make sure he doesn't hear you. He still believes in Santa Claus, you know."

"Yeah, I know. Not to worry. The boy's outside."

I savored her scorn. Better to be scowled at than ignored—the reason I deliberately left my coffee cups on the counter. Might as well add fuel to the fire. "Belle Thompson helped me pick out the bike."

Penny never said a bad word about anyone she'd ever met. I'd hoped to make my wife jealous—proof she still cared what I did. She never complained when I'd come home slightly buzzed. I blamed my inebriated state on her. If she'd come back to my bed, I'd become a teetotaler. She slammed the dishwasher door. At this stage, her rage felt like a lukewarm kiss, not hot enough to satisfy but better than silence. Since anger never stayed long in Penny's heart, she returned her attention to kitchen matters.

Not adept in a place I considered Mom and Penny's domain, I felt edged out of the kitchen. Any other day when frigid temps inside matched those outside, I'd head out to Belle's. She never failed to entertain with her slam-dunk philosophies about life. Not today. Millie's anticipated arrival spurred a bigger challenge than a Christmas Eve dinner. I needed to know why Millie ran away and why my father deserted us. Mom held the answers to both questions. It'd take a pair of mental pliers to pull the truth out of her.

I picked up her highness' photograph. Mom grabbed the frame from my grasp and returned it to its mantel throne before she resumed her more pleasant tasks. I covered a giggle as she dumped flour into the sifter, the puff like a white cloud of resistance.

This time, I balked. "Mom, don't shove me away like a little kid any longer. I need to know what happened to Millie ... and my father. I insist. You owe me."

My mother's eyes filled with tears while Penny stuffed the bird. I sensed their shared glances as if Penny already knew the secrets my mother kept from me. If Mom could confide in a daughter-in-law, why did she ignore the pleas of her only child? Unless I had caused my father to leave.

Mom dropped the mixing bowl, its rattle against the counter a rebuttal in and of itself. "What does one have to do with the other?"

"Every instinct tells me they're connected. It's time you told me how."

She brought me a cup of coffee then sat next to me, her glare a signal I'd won this battle. "Okay. You sit, too, Penny. The truth is long overdue."

Penny's eyes widened. Like Blackie's eyes ... my pet mutt. The best friend a boy could have. His love covered me when I had none from either parent. One day I found him caught in a bear trap after we'd taken a hike in the woods, his eyes wide with panic as his life slipped away. What was Penny afraid of? She sat next to me. I reached for her hand, but she pulled it away.

A cold wind followed R.J.'s energetic entrance.

"Shut the door, Sonny," I scolded.

He pushed it closed with his booted foot. "Sorry, Daddy. Come outside with me. I built an ice castle. I think I'll call it Fort McDougal."

R.J. loved to build things. I sat tall in the chair. No way could I leave this child. If need be, I'd learn to manage without Penny's love.

But, I'd sooner die than face a day without R.J.—the only hope that moored me to Maple Street.

"That's a great idea, R.J. I'll be out in a bit to take a look. The grownups need to talk first."

"I know. When grownups talk, kids need to get deaf." He went back outside. R.J. had his project to deal with, and I had mine. "Okay, Mom. Let's hear it."

She went to the living room, then returned with Millie's portrait. She held it as she talked. "Millie was more than my cousin. She was the best friend I ever had."

"I figured as much."

"We were like sisters." Mom reached for a tissue. "I'll try not to hold back the truth. But I'm afraid."

"Of what?"

"I don't want you to hate me."

Penny held my mother's hand, two women joined in their mutual secrets.

A bear goes deeper into his cave when he senses nature is about to throw a temper tantrum. I wasn't as smart as a woodland creature. I had to know. "Go ahead, Mom. Nothing you say will make me hate you."

Bertie
March
1961

Millie brushed her long, midnight colored hair, so thick it fell in complete obedience over her shoulders. I watched as she counted every stroke, my yawn well-earned.

Finally, she stopped long enough to toss a pile of 45s to me, her aim short of the bed. The whole lot dotted the carpet with black vinyl. I sorted the bundle by performer and title, except for the Elvis collection. They weren't mine. Still, Elvis deserved to be on top.

I declared my fanatic devotion. "I love Elvis."

Millie scowled—the way she showed disapproval. "For his talent or his wavy hair?" We might be cousins, but our preferences were at opposite ends of any given spectrum. Maybe those differences eventually shredded our love for each other. At fifteen, we believed we'd never be separated.

Millie set her brush on her vanity. "Don't see what all the fuss is about where Elvis is concerned. Talent is not determined by a person's looks … singers or actors."

I walked over to Millie's phonograph, then put on *Love Me Tender*, *A Teenager in Love*, and *Will You Still Love Me Tomorrow*. "You'll like these."

She shrugged and resumed brushing her hair. I thought maybe she'd brush herself bald—a hundred strokes every afternoon with another session before she went to bed. She never cheated on the count. If a hydrogen bomb went off, Millie would still make sure she got in every last stroke before she took cover.

I combed my straight, mousy brown hair twice a day—only enough to get the snarls out.

She sighed then put her brush back on the vanity. "There. Done."

"About time."

She wrinkled her nose like a rabbit, so I'd know she wasn't really mad. "What's on television tonight? It's your turn to choose what we watch."

"I don't know."

"Bertie, you're as decisive as a caged animal—back and forth with no destination in mind. I think *Perry Mason* is on?"

"Perry never loses, and his clients are never guilty. Let's watch *Bonanza*. I love Little Joe. He sorta looks like Elvis."

Millie's face contorted into a full-blown frown.

In self-defense, I returned her glare. Seemed these days, Millie found fault with everything I did—she'd become my sole judge and jury. Since she would find fault anyway, I might as well do what I wanted. She could pound rock salt for all I cared. Only, I did care. I didn't want her to know how much her scowls hurt me.

"Bertie, you're incorrigible." Millie threw around five syllable words like confetti.

"At least I don't try to impress people with long words. What does incorrigible mean, anyway?"

"Incurably bad."

"So you think I'm bad?"

"That's what I said."

"Mama thinks I'm bad too, only she doesn't use words like incorrigible. Her words aren't proper to repeat."

I didn't want to stay on the topic of my mother, so I reached for my life-size poster of Elvis. I held it like a dance partner as I swayed to the music. The cutout and a few stuffed animals were the only possessions I brought when I moved in with Uncle Walter.

"Bertie, stop dancing. Daddy can't stand Elvis. Says it's unnatural the way his hips gyrate."

I didn't see why I couldn't dance the way I wanted in the privacy of our rooms. Between the two of us, Millie was the only one who believed in rules, obedient even when no one watched.

"Fine," I said then plopped to the floor as I re-sorted Millie's hundreds of records—only a dozen rock and roll, my favorite. Millie liked classical music. When she hit a high note, I looked to see if glass shattered. Nothing broke although I worried my eardrums had ruptured.

When the records were put back into the case, Millie put it into her closet while I took my turn at the vanity. I shaped my strands into stubby angel wings. "Any ideas as to what I can do with this mess?"

"Bertie, you have beautiful hair. You shouldn't be so negative about yourself."

Millie whisked my hair into a twist. "I like it this way. Accentuates your slender neckline."

I pushed her hands away then made a pretend fist. "If you use another big word, I swear; I'll give you a black eye." I took out a rat-tail comb, dipped it in styling lotion then rolled my hair up in the brushed curlers I'd bought with the most recent guilt money from Mama. She mailed twenty dollars every month. I was supposed to give most of it to Uncle Walter to pay for my keep. The rest I could spend as I wanted. Uncle Walter refused to take any money from Mama, so I saved what I didn't need. If I saved enough by the time I turned sixteen, I hoped to hop on a bus for New York City to become an actress.

With my hair rolled up, I searched for Millie's hairdryer. "Where did you stash the torture chamber today? You never put stuff back in the same place."

"Try the hall closet."

When I returned, Millie sat at the vanity and stared vacantly into the mirror, as if in a trance. She called her episodes daydreams. To me, she looked as though she went into another world altogether. Whatever place she went to seemed real enough to her—a place I wished I could visit. Her zone-outs still annoyed me. She'd go off to her perfect worlds and leave me in this crazy one. After two minutes, she shook herself back to reality.

"Where to this time? College?"

She shrugged her shoulders. "I was thinking about an article I read yesterday."

"About what?"

"Not what. Who."

"Who, then?"

"Eleanor Roosevelt."

"Yeah?" Both of us liked to read. Only Millie read about politics, while I read about movie stars.

"She's been assigned by President Kennedy to get more women into high-level government offices. She's convinced him to start a commission to study women's equality in the workplace, especially government. Finally, a president who appreciates what women can contribute to society."

Impressed, I tried to whistle. My gallant attempts only resulted in spit. I could sing, but I couldn't whistle, not like Papa. I missed how he whistled happy songs every morning while he shaved. I wiped my mouth then warbled my opinion instead. "So why don't you become a politician? You'd be a good one since you constantly preach women should be treated the same as men."

"They should."

"Mama doesn't think so. She says if God wanted men and women to be the same, he'd have given men breasts and women—"

"Bertie!"

"God made men and women different for a reason. We shouldn't mess up what God intended."

Millie laughed. Not a polite snort as if I'd she understood my joke. Her laughs lately had become more like taunts. "Since when did you become religious?"

"I'm not religious. I agree with Mama, men should be men and women should be women."

"I think a woman should be able to go into any profession she desires—even be a cop or a firefighter."

"There's a reason they're called police*men* and fire*men*."

"Bertie, you're so ignorant. Society can change what they call them. Gender shouldn't be an issue."

I laughed so hard it came straight up from my toes. "No wonder Uncle Walter doesn't want you to go to college. Not with ideas like those in your head."

"Daddy's as narrow-minded as Aunt Donna. He doesn't think girls should go to college at all. He wants both of us to marry farmers so we'll stay in Cold Creek for the rest of our lives."

Not what I wanted for my future any more than Millie. She could be anything she wanted. "Uncle Walter's proud of you, although he worries a lot. I overheard him tell Peter Hannigan how worried he was about you."

"What did he say?"

I had a knack for mimicry, the one trait Millie still liked about me. So I acted out her father's conversation. "He said 'Peter, someday my little girl will leave me to go to college. Gonna be lonely here with just Jonas to keep me company. He nags me worse than ten wives.'"

Millie smiled. "You sounded exactly like Daddy."

I reached for the most recent issue of *American Girl*, thumbing its pages until I found the article on how to be a good listener on a date.

Millie snatched the magazine from my hands, lifted the bonnet on the hairdryer, and shouted into my ear. "I heard Skip Bilow will be at the matinée tomorrow. Want to go?"

"What do you think? That I like to go through all this trouble for no reason?"

"Then it's true, you like him?"

I couldn't figure out why she asked such a dumb question. Everyone in our high school knew I liked Skip Bilow. "Why do you ask?"

"If you don't like him, maybe I'll go after him for a boyfriend."

Sometimes Millie's mean spirit made Mama seem like a pushover. I flipped off the bonnet, stormed to Millie's bed and spit a few swear words as I dropped down face first. "Millie Cooper, if you weren't my best friend in the world, I'd beat you up. You know I like Skip Bilow. If he thinks you like him, he'll never give me the time of day."

My mother's meanness came from a cesspool of disappointment, but Millie's scorn came from a different place. She never meant to be unkind—her teases more like wind gusts that caught me off guard. Still, the fact I understood why Millie scratched at my spirit didn't ease the pain.

She sat next to me. "Don't cry, Bertie. I meant it as a joke. I'm not interested in Skip Bilow. He's definitely not my type."

What type would interest Millie Cooper? I never saw her walk with boys in the halls nor did any boy from school call her on the phone. Skip Bilow walked me to my locker more than once. Sometimes he'd kiss me. Didn't boys only kiss girls they liked?

I sat up on the bed. "Cross your heart and hope to die?"

She drew the letter *x* across her chest. "Now stop crying. I don't like it when you cry."

I wiped my eyes with my blouse sleeve. "I'd never steal your boyfriend."

Millie laughed. "Well, I don't have one, so I guess I'll never know."

"Unless you have a secret one."

"We should make a pact." Millie dashed to her dresser then pulled out a white leather Bible. "This was my mother's. Now look at me, square in the eyes."

I tried to be serious even though a pinky promise to each other seemed as ridiculous as a talking horse.

"Raise your right hand, then put your left one on this Bible."

"Like in *Perry Mason*?"

"Yes. Like in *Perry Mason*."

"Mama says it's a sin to swear on the Bible."

Millie growled as she placed the Bible on the vanity, went to her bookcase and returned with a copy of *Gone with the Wind*. "We'll pretend this is a Bible. Since it's not real, it won't be a sin."

I placed my hand on her book. "Okay, Harvard. I promise to tell the truth, the whole truth, and nothing but the truth."

She smiled. "Repeat after me—"

"Repeat after me."

Millie offered a loud, drawn-out sigh.

"Sorry."

"I solemnly swear."

"I solemnly swear …"

The whole scene tickled me like someone had put a feather against my nose. I held my stomach to stay steady as the belly laughs echoed through the room.

Millie squared her shoulders. "Stop it!"

"This is stupid!"

"Stupid, huh?" Millie hit my back with her pillow.

"Hey. Are there rocks in there?"

"No. I have a good aim."

"Watch out for payback." I returned fire.

The pretend war might have turned serious if Uncle Walter hadn't shouted upstairs. "You girls quit foolin' around up there. Sounds like the floor's about to collapse."

Millie leaned over the rail. "Sorry, Daddy. We'll quiet down."

Uncle Walter always sounded stern though I knew he wasn't really upset. I loved Uncle Walter like he was my own father. When Papa died, Uncle Walter wrapped his arm around my shoulder. "I'll try to do right by you, Bertie. A girl needs a father in her life." Far as I was concerned, Uncle Walter could holler at me all he wanted. His yell sounded more like a lullaby.

"Time to set the table for supper. I'll need to go back to the barn for a quick chore then we'll eat."

Since Uncle Walter made few demands, when he gave an order, no one argued. All discussion over Skip Bilow came to an abrupt end. I figured if Millie had her sights on Skip, I might as well find some other boy to like. All the boys were crazy about Millie Cooper, but she wouldn't give the go sign to any of them.

I yanked the curlers out of my hair, then we danced down the steps to *A Teenager in Love*. I jabbered about how Dion and the Belmonts could have been killed in the same crash as Buddy Holly. "I'm sure glad he decided the plane ticket cost too much money, aren't you?"

Millie didn't answer. She'd drifted off to another place, out of my reach until she decided to come back to Cold Creek again. After a few minutes, the trance ended, and she took off on another road. "I'm worried about Daddy."

"How so?"

"He needs to start planting soon."

I understood about farms. My older brothers worked for Uncle Walter until Verne left town for places unknown and John joined the Army, most likely to get away from Mama.

"Since your brothers left, Daddy tries to do all the work by himself. His arthritis is so bad I don't know how he manages to keep up on his own."

I shared Millie's worry. Jonas was no help in the barn. City bred, he never did figure out how to use a milking machine. He preferred to take care of the house and keep an eye on us girls.

The war in Southeast Asia had ramped up. Seemed more and more young men got drafted or volunteered each month. Good farm hands were hard to find.

"Even if he could find help, he can't afford to pay much. Daddy is afraid he'll have to sell the farm like Gary Johnson. He was fourth generation, too."

Finally, a current event topic I knew something about. I swelled with pride at my scant bit of knowledge. Millie already knew, but I wanted to show her I could read a newspaper as good as she could. "I read milk prices fell again. These days the small farmer can barely break even, why, so many take on the risk of too much debt in order to expand. Can't survive on status quo."

Millie's eyes bugged. "Bertie Brown, sometimes you amaze me. You're really one of the smartest girls I know. I don't understand why you don't like school."

"Don't need mathematics to be an actress."

Millie could dart from thought to thought faster than Clark Kent turned into Superman. When I looked, her eyes filled with tears.

"No need to cry. You know I've always hated school."

She drew her lips into a half smile. "Sometimes I wished I'd been born a boy so Daddy would let me help him in the barn. He thinks a girl's place is in the house."

I could follow an opera easier than carry on a conversation with Millie.

"You worry way too much. Uncle Walter will find some help soon. They're always drifters who need work. Uncle Walter is right. Farming is a job for men."

Millie unfurled the tablecloth onto Aunt Margaret's old oak table. "Jonas stays in the house instead of milking. I can't understand why the rules say the man has to work, and the woman has to cook. My mother helped Daddy with chores."

"Uncle Walter doesn't want you in the barn because he's afraid you'll get sick like Aunt Margaret did."

"My mother died of pneumonia not because she worked in the barn. A storm knocked out the electricity. She'd have been just as cold in the house."

Millie went to the hutch next to the gun cabinet then brought over a stack of plates. I didn't mind any kind of housework, but I froze when I came near the gun cabinet. I could still see Papa as he lay dead on the ground, his chest busted open by a rifle bullet. When he hadn't come home from hunting, Mama made me and my brothers look for him. Since then, I couldn't go near a gun.

I sighed at Millie's haphazard way she set the table—forks on the wrong side of the plate and glasses put at random angles. "That's all wrong, and you know it."

Maybe she set the table every which way but right to get me mad enough to take over.

"The glass goes precisely by the tip of the knife, and the knife blade has to be turned so it faces the plate. The plates have to be exactly two inches from the edge of the table. If I don't set the table the right way, Mama slaps my hand so hard it welts up."

Millie hugged the breath right out of me.

"What's with the hug?"

"I thought you needed one."

"Well, I don't." I never got hugs after my father died, except from Millie. Mama didn't know how to touch except with Papa's horse reins.

Jonas came in from the kitchen, his spatula held out like a spear. "A sloth would've had the table set by now. Hurry it up. Meatloaf's done. I don't want it ruined because of you two slow pokes."

I reset the last knife. "We're done, Jonas."

"Go get Walter." Jonas went back to the kitchen. He barked orders like a drill sergeant as if he expected us to hop to his command. When his back was turned, we girls saluted simultaneously.

We raced to the barn. "Soups on," we shouted together.

Uncle Walter washed his hands in the milk house sink. "I'll shower and be up shortly. Might as well quit for the day. That heifer ain't quite ready to birth. Afraid it'll be a breach. Can't afford vet bills, and I can't afford to lose any more livestock." He turned toward the sound of crushed gravel. "Probably Pete. Could set my clock by his arrivals. Go on up to the house and set another plate."

Since Peter Hannigan's wife died, he'd become a frequent guest. When Uncle Walter came up from the barn, everyone sat then filled their plate while he, Jonas, and Peter Hannigan talked politics, mostly about President Kennedy.

"I might be a Republican, but I voted for him," Uncle Walter said.

Peter Hannigan scratched his beard. "Then what you got against John Boy now?"

"Hate his Southeast Asia policy. Our boys are being slaughtered like pigs on Friday over there. No easy fix, either. Before all is said and done, we'll be entrenched in an unwinnable war."

Jonas went to the kitchen and returned with apple pie and coffee. After dessert, the men went into the living room while we girls did the dishes.

From the snatches of conversation we overheard, Uncle Walter complained about the last Grange meeting. "Sure enough, when I've served this term as president, I'll hand the gavel over. I've more than done my duty."

I figured Uncle Walter was about to perform his daily tribute to Jonas. I never tired of the story so I hid behind the door to listen and mouthed the words in sync as Uncle Walter delivered his monolog. "Jonas and me were Army buddies. When my Margaret died, I took to the bottle. Jonas came to visit and found me so drunk I couldn't take care of my little Millie. He got me sobered up and decided to stay on to keep me that way. I saved his life in France, he saved mine in Cold Creek." Then he lifted his one-glass-limit of wine to make a toast. "Here's to the day I started to live again."

Mama thought eavesdropping was a sin. One day, she discovered I'd listened in on the phone while she talked with Reverend Jacobs about Linda Hastings' out-of-wedlock pregnancy. "No one likes an eavesdropper," she screamed. "Some conversations aren't fit for young girls to hear." She got so angry she pushed me against the kitchen counter then slapped me a dozen times across the face.

I ran off to Uncle Walter's house with my Elvis cutout in tow. When he opened the door, all he said was, "This is your home now, Bertie."

I felt happy at Uncle Walter's house, a place where people gave hugs instead of slaps. Uncle Walter and Jonas acted like an old married couple. Not like Bob and Keith who lived down the road. Folks knew they had relations with each other. Uncle Walter and Jonas both dated women. I expected one day, one or the other would take a wife. For now, they seemed to be content with status quo.

I felt a soft snap on my behind then turned. "Bertie Brown, you know better than to eavesdrop." As he normally did, Jonas laughed after he toweled me then rejoined the men in the other room, bringing in dessert. Careful to stay out of sight, I leaned close to the archway.

Peter Hannigan took a sip of his wine then said, "Walter, Millie's one pretty girl. Aren't you worried about her and boys?"

Uncle Walter half laughed, half groaned. "I tell you, Pete, I'm proud of my girl. She plans to go to college. I do worry, though. She'll be sixteen on Christmas Eve. I know I should warn her about guys like us."

Ryan
Christmas Eve
1999

The timer captured Mom's attention while I was left to wonder why she'd never mentioned her Uncle Walter before, a man I'd like to know.

As was her habit, Mom explained her every move. "Need to get busy with preparations. I want dinner and dishes done when Millie gets here so we have plenty of time to visit. I have to make sure I make R.J. the whipped cream he asked for."

A part of me resented the attention she showered on R.J. Yet, another part was grateful Mom had found purpose again. How she loved him. She used to dote on me in a long ago memory. If not for R.J., I suppose she'd still be stuck in front of the kitchen window in the vain hope her man would come back.

We all turned at the thud. "What was that?" Mom asked. She knew as well as I did a screen had come loose. She never asked me to fix stuff. Instead, she posed her request in the form of an investigative question.

"I promised R.J. I'd take a look at his fort. I'll take care of the screen while I'm out there." I put on my jacket and cap. "I expect you'll tell me the rest when I come back in?"

Mom nodded as I went outside. While I righted the screen, I glanced at Penny who stared outside, her gaze fixed on an object beyond me. I followed her gaze to an old maple tree. Lots of them on our road—how it got its name. A leaf stubbornly hung from barren branches. A rare sight this late in December. Was I like that leaf? A man who clung to the hopeless?

I anchored the screen then lifted my collar to fight the cold wind. R.J. played with his trucks. He had lined them up in precise rows as if he'd taken a ruler to measure the space between the vehicles. He picked up his toy radio. "Commando One calling Commando Two. Do you read me, Commando Two? Over."

I pretended to have an intercom in my hand. "Copy that, Commando One. This is Commando Two. There's a big storm on the horizon. Take immediate cover. Over."

R.J.'s smiles made me feel like a hero, and I puffed with pride to think, at least in his eyes, I was invincible."

"Hi, Daddy."

"Whadda up to, Sonny?"

He shook his head like I'd asked a dumb question. "Playing, of course."

"What ya got there."

"A convoy. That's a funny word. Why do they call it a convoy?"

While in the Army, I earned the equivalent of an associate degree in criminal justice, and I considered myself of above average intelligence. Even so, R.J. asked questions that would stump Einstein. If I didn't know the answer, I changed the subject.

"Let's play catch."

"In the snow?"

"Sure. It'll be fun."

"Deal."

"Pick up your toys while I get our gear."

I kept my equipment in the house but had a set from my childhood I stored in the shed a few years back to save for when R.J. was a little bigger. Almost old enough now. Why not? Guilt came over me anytime I went near the shed, so I purposefully stored most of my stuff in the garage along with lawn care equipment. Penny had nagged me for almost a year to build one. When a man loves a woman, he should get right on any request she makes. What she'd asked wasn't difficult. I complained the whole while I worked on it. From then on, Penny didn't ask me to do another home improvement. Was this the reason she didn't love me anymore? Had I become as indifferent to her as she had to me?

The door stuck on what looked like an old Polaroid photograph I assumed had fallen from one of the boxes stored above. Gina Forbes chided me about my unhealthy curiosity. "Ryan, not every riddle needs to be solved," she'd said. I should have listened. However, squirrels climb trees, and Ryan McDougal can't let a mystery alone.

From the stage, I knew the picture had been taken at the Oasis nightclub. The faces were scribbled over with thick black strokes. Did R.J. do this? The girl in the cowgirl outfit had to be Penny. The man on the far right was Declan Peterson, the lead guitarist. He towered a foot above everyone else. The other two men wore identical shirts—probably Chris Tooley, the drummer, and Lane Brandt, bass guitarist. The figure by the bar had been beheaded as if someone tried to cut him out of the picture. Based on the expensive suit, I figured it had to be the owner, Gavin Blackwell.

I reached up to put it away when I noticed Penny's iridescent crate stuffed in a far corner. I recognized it as the one she'd used to pack her memorabilia when I moved her out of her apartment onto the base after we got married. When I brought my family to Granite Falls, she'd stored it in the attic. I wasn't surprised the crate had been moved. I only marveled at its condition, as if someone had deliberately smashed it.

Married not quite a week after we met, the fact we were strangers didn't matter. I figured we had a lifetime to get to know one another. Though she resisted most questions about her past, I managed to learn her parents had been killed in a car accident. After they had died, Penny had lived with a despised elderly aunt. She moved in with Declan's family at the age of sixteen.

The picture made me suddenly more curious about her earlier life. Why did she destroy her memories? I pocketed the photograph, grabbed my second-hand baseball gear then closed the shed door. I'd ask Penny about the picture later. Right now my son waited patiently for a game of catch with his hero dad.

I learned how to play baseball from a juvenile cop, Officer John Doty, a man who felt sorry for me. He took over where a father should have been in my life. I promised myself if I ever had a son he wouldn't have to learn how to throw a baseball from anyone else but his dad.

After a few lobs, R.J. stopped. He gazed upward, his face twisted with concern. "Daddy, who's the best baseball player?"

"You mean now?"

"Ever."

No way could I dodge this one and expect my son to still believe I was the smartest man in the world. After a few more tosses, I came up with an answer. "There have been a lot of great baseball players over the years, like Babe Ruth. If I have to pick the player I most admire, I'd have to say, Cal Ripken Jr."

"Why?"

"Because he's consistently showed up to play. Will probably have a record of most consecutive games played."

"Why is that a good thing?"

"He keeps showing up even when he doesn't feel like it. As far as I'm concerned, he's the most faithful player who ever wore a baseball uniform."

"What else did he do?"

"He won a lot of other awards, but he's best known for his loyalty."

R.J. scrunched his face into a question mark.

"His team knows they can depend on him. He shows up to play even if he's in a slump or when the fans boo him when he strikes out."

R.J. shrugged. "And that makes him a great player?"

"Absolutely." My arm gave out long before R.J.'s energy. The weatherman forecasted overnight temperatures below zero, and the thermometer dipped rapidly. "I'm cold."

"Can I stay outside?"

"Maybe for a little longer."

"Deal."

"Besides, I think tomorrow is a special day. I can't remember what it is, though."

He always managed to call my bluff. "Daddy, you know."

"Oh, right, Christmas. What do you hope Santa will bring?"

"I want a bike like the one I showed you and Aunt Belle."

"Well, now, are you big enough for a bike?"

"Sure. I'm six, remember?"

While I returned the gear to the shed, R.J. rolled in the snow toward his imaginary convoy. I envied the power of children to live in make-believe worlds. If not for the insatiable desire to know what happened to Millie and my father, I'd have stayed in R.J.'s fantasies despite the cold.

Penny peeled potatoes at the counter while Mom wiped off the table. I poured myself a cup of freshly brewed coffee and tapped my feet while I gulped it down, unable to hide my impatience. I always suspected Mom busied herself with housework to avoid conversation much like I took off to Belle's when life came at me.

I fumbled the crumpled photograph in my pocket. Could this explain, at least partially, why my wife despised me? Did she blame me her career had been cut short? I never told her to quit, and I would have supported her if she'd decided to stay with the band. She handed me her crate then said, "Those days are over for good." Maybe now, she regretted her decision.

After all the noble lies were unmasked, this naked flaw screeched at me. I was not the Cal Ripken of husbands I pretended to me. I didn't want to talk to Penny about the picture for fear I'd subconsciously kept her from her dreams. To save our marriage, I'd convince her to sing again, if that's what she wanted. First, though, I needed to pull more truth out of my mother's album of regrets. This time, I wouldn't let her retreat until I connected the dots from Millie's disappearance to my father's abandonment, no matter how much ugliness I unearthed in the process.

As a youth, I envied my friends who celebrated Christmas with relatives. For the first time in my life, my mother mentioned family I never knew. My father was an only child, and his parents died shortly after I was born. Were any of Mom's family still alive? If so, why didn't she ever mention them?

Millie's was the only picture Mom displayed. While storing items in the attic, I discovered a box of old photographs. Some of them were pictures of people I didn't recognize. In one, Mom stood next to an older couple and two teenage boys. The inscription on the back read *Easter, 1955*. Everyone looked happy. I guessed the boys were Mom's brothers, while the couple must have been her parents. Earlier, Mom mentioned her father died during a hunting accident. She never talked about Grandma Brown. What happened to tear this family apart?

I also found two obituaries in the box—one for a John Brown, killed in Vietnam, predeceased by his father, Norman Brown, the only survivor, his mother, Donna Brown. No mention of Mom or the other brother, Verne. The second obituary was for Donna Cooper Brown. No mention of any survivors or any relatives who might have predeceased her. Strange. Mom's name had been left out of both. I wondered why she kept them.

As I remembered the treasure trove of memorabilia, I was filled with a new sense of urgency. Mom must finish her story. Perhaps my mother believed past events, especially painful ones, were best left buried. I needed answers, and if I were to know the whole truth, I'd have to draw the facts out as cautiously as a beekeeper extracts honey.

If Mom wouldn't come to me, I'd join her world. I grabbed a towel, dried a plate, and opened the cupboard above me. As I put the dish away, my mother yanked it from my hand. "The dinner dishes go in the other cupboard, Ryan."

If need be, I'd extract the story one dish at a time. "So Mom, did Uncle Walter hire help or did he sell the farm?" Seemed like an innocent question.

Mom grabbed my dishtowel and threw it on the counter. "Since you are so determined to drag the story out of me, sit down."

I obeyed.

Tears filled her eyes as she sat. "Uncle Walter hired a drifter by the name of Stoney Rivers."

Bertie
April
1961

No girl could have been happier at the end of a weekday than I was. Not so for Millie. School gave her purpose as she formed her goals. Millie Cooper would change the world. As soon as we got off the bus, she rushed to the barn, eager to spew the events of her day to Uncle Walter. I trailed behind and would much rather have grabbed one of Jonas' brownies before I lied to Uncle Walter. I couldn't tell him how Mr. Adams yelled at me for incomplete assignments or how I'd failed another math test.

The day Stoney Rivers came Millie met me half way back to the house before I'd even reached the barn. "Daddy's not here. He always milks about this time. I hope nothing's wrong."

Millie worried over Uncle Walter even more than he worried about her. You could fill the Grand Canyon with the worries those two had for one another.

"Doesn't mean trouble," I said.

We ambled into the kitchen, filled with the scent of freshly baked cherry pie. Uncle Walter sauntered in from the den and sniffed the air. "Smells wonderful, Jonas. Don't suppose you'd let us all have an early dessert? Maybe more coffee, too?"

"Coming right up." While Jonas made the coffee, he whistled *Amazing Grace*.

Uncle Walter sat on a stool. He eyed Millie like Hamilton Burger, the prosecutor on *Perry Mason*. "So how was school today?"

While Millie spewed about her accomplishments, I took time to fabricate my story. She took longer to report since she rambled on about her new friends, Mary and Veronica, how smart they were, how they also hoped to go to Harvard.

Millie's classes seemed like a waste of time, except for her honors English course. She studied Shakespeare. I liked to read plays, even hard to understand ones like Shakespeare. When I read romance novels, I'd pretend to be the heroine and act out the story when no one could see me. The guidance counselor said I wasn't college material. The best I could hope for was a job as a waitress or maybe a department store clerk. He recommended I focus on home economics for when I got married.

We rode the bus together—the only part of school we shared. The college-bound classes were on the third floor while mine were mainly in the vocational wing.

Millie poured two glasses of milk then handed me one like I was a guest. She bubbled with worry as she glanced toward Uncle Walter. "Why weren't you in the barn? What's wrong?"

Uncle Walter perked up. "Don't get nervous. I have good news. I interviewed a young man who Jonas recommended."

Millie glared at Jonas. "You recommended help to my father when you can't even operate a milking machine?"

He took out a server for the pie. "I saw him by the side of the road with his thumb in the air so I offered him a ride. I asked him where he wanted to go. 'Anywhere I can get work,' he said. Said he was originally from Idaho. He's had a bunch of odd jobs. Wants to go to New York City eventually."

Millie put her glass on the counter. She stayed calm, but her eyes gleamed with scorn. "Daddy, I don't believe you. You hired somebody off the street, without references?"

Uncle Walter laughed. "I thought Jonas was as good a reference as the boy needed."

"Does this boy have a name?"

"Stoney Rivers."

Millie growled. "Sounds made up to me."

Jonas served pie all the way around. "Probably is. The kid wants to be an actor. Seems to be an amiable sort. The way I see it, he needs a job, and Walter needs help. Sounds like a fix for both their problems."

Millie pushed her pie to the side. "How do you know he's not an ax murderer or a runaway fugitive?"

Uncle Walter poured himself a cup of coffee. "Not your place to judge who I hire. The boy will do fine."

I downed my pie as I conjured what this Stoney Rivers might look like. Uncle Walter called him a boy, but I supposed anyone under thirty might seem like a boy to him.

Millie refused to let the matter go. "He has to be a crazy person. Only crazy people go to New York City."

Did Millie lump me among those crazy people since all I ever wanted to do was be an actress?

"What about farm experience?" Millie asked.

Jonas started in on his piece of pie. "He said he's a migrant farm worker. Problem is there hasn't been much farm work available this winter."

"Great. So you've hired a stranger from Idaho who wants to be an actor and probably has never milked a cow. He won't stay long. He'll be gone with his first paycheck. Where is he?"

"Just needed the bathroom for a minute. He'll be here for your quick examination soon enough." Uncle Walter stood, his face wrinkled with disdain. "The boy promised to stay through the end of the year if I'd give him a job. Says he can drive a tractor. He's built solid so I expect he can lift hay. He'll earn his keep. I'll teach him how to milk and hay. Jonas is the only man I know who couldn't figure out how to milk a cow. Besides, I either hire help or sell. Far as I can see, Stoney Rivers is a godsend."

"Or a curse," Millie said. "Which do you think he is, Bertie?"

"Time will tell." I gulped down my milk then picked up my math book. I never looked at it. I only brought it home to impress Uncle Walter. I nearly collided with the tall man who came into the kitchen. Millie's eyes bugged at his confident swagger. Even I knew he didn't get that walk on a potato farm. Dressed in a tight tee and fitted jeans and with his long black hair swept into a ponytail, Peter Hannigan might have labeled Stony a beatnik. He was no boy, either—his five o'clock shadow covered his face.

A worn duffel bag hung over his right shoulder. "Thanks for the job, Mr. Cooper. I won't let you down." His deep voice reminded me of Johnny Cash. I wondered if he was musical as well as an actor.

Uncle Walter finished his last bite of pie. "I'm sure we'll get along fine. This is my daughter, Millie. The one with the math book tight to her chest that I know darn well she never looks at is my niece, Bertie. She's a boarder here since last summer."

Stoney's perfect smile revealed a set of even white teeth. I understood actors needed to have nice smiles. Stoney's was way above nice. "If someone will show me to my room, I'll be out to the barn as soon as I unpack."

"Ambitious. A quality I admire. Millie, show Stoney around the house. I thought he could bunk where Bertie's brothers used to sleep."

Millie bristled. "Fine. This way, Mr. Rivers." She headed toward the steps with Stoney not far behind.

When God made Stoney Rivers, he went overboard as far as looks were concerned. Firm muscles bulged underneath his tee. If he didn't do much farm work, he must work out.

Jonas gave me a shove toward the steps. "Go help Millie get Stoney settled. Sooner he unpacks, the sooner he can get to work."

I walked into John and Verne's old room as Millie threw a top sheet onto the lower bunk. "Bertie, grab a set of towels from the hall closet." When I came back, Stoney had already taken ownership of John's old dresser. Millie pointed down the hall. "The fastest way to the kitchen is by the back stairwell. The fastest way to the barn is through the kitchen."

Stoney leaned against the doorframe, a little closer to Millie than a stranger should. I wished it was me in the doorway instead of Millie. "Nice house."

She rattled non-stop about the Cooper Homestead. I thought how Mama lived here as a little girl before she married Papa. Too bad she and Uncle Walter couldn't see eye to eye.

Millie went full speed ahead. "The original house was built around 1810 by our ancestor, Simon Cooper, the first Cooper to come to Cold Creek from England. This room, as well as the two adjacent rooms, were used as servant headquarters. The field hands stayed in a bunk house. It burned down fifty years ago. Of course, the barn is modernized, especially after the invention of the milk machine … by a woman, I might add."

"Truth?" Stoney asked.

"Anna Baldwin patented it," I added.

"L.O. Colvin engineered it," Millie said before I could. Didn't she know when she showed off her smarts she made me look dumb?

Stoney gazed around the room. "Nice digs. Does the fireplace still work?"

Millie plopped an extra set of sheets into Verne's dresser. "Afraid not. There's no closet in this room. You'll have to use the hooks on the back of the door." She closed it some so Stoney could see what she meant. "My father showers in the barn before supper, so you'll want to keep a change of clothes there. Daddy puts his barn clothes into plastic bags then brings them to the house for Jonas to launder. As you can see, there's no smell in this house. We'd like to keep it that way."

I wondered at Millie's snootiness. She was friendly to most guests, especially Peter Hannigan who was like family as far as we were concerned. "We have several bathrooms. You'll use the full bath at the end of the hall next to Jonas' room. Bertie and I sleep in the rooms across the hall."

I expected Millie to say we were like Siamese Twins, where one went the other went and most of the time we slept in the same room, either hers or mine. Maybe she didn't because we went back to our own rooms after she found her new friends.

Stoney put on a cap then slung a change of clothes over his arm. "What I got on will do for the barn. I should hurry so I can help Walter."

Millie and Stoney locked stares, like kids in a dare, until he blinked and leaned against the wall, his gaze fixed on Millie's silky hair. "I'm sure I'll feel at home in no time."

Millie crossed her arms. "How old are you, Mr. Rivers? I'd guess twenty-one or twenty-two?"

"Turned twenty-two last month." He leaned in and smiled. "Please, drop the Mr. Rivers bit. The name's Stoney."

"Your real name?"

He laughed. "Actually, yes. Stone Jacob Rivers is my given name." This time, he took a step toward me, so close I could smell his cologne ... Stetson, the brand Papa wore.

I'd have stayed in the moment if Millie hadn't pulled me by the arm. We headed back downstairs. Stoney trailed behind like a puppy after its master. As he talked with Jonas and Uncle Walter, his laugh changed. I thought of Verne who had two laughs. One was careful, especially around grownups. The other he used with girls.

"Will I see you at dinner?"

I wasn't sure who the question was for since Millie and I stood next to each other.

I struck the same pose as Marilyn Monroe in *Some Like it Hot*. "I expect so." My antics garnered a warm smile.

As Stoney left, Millie slapped me gently on the wrist, but hard enough it stung. "Bertie Brown you acted abominably."

"I am not ... whatever the word means."

"It means you acted like a trollop around Mr. Rivers."

"He said to call him Stoney. Besides, I only meant to be friendly. He's a stranger. Mama says whoever is kind to a stranger earns a place in heaven. It's in the Bible."

"I'm not very religious, Bertie, but I think it's worded a little differently."

"Mama knows her Bible so it must be right. Anyway, Stoney is harmless. What does it matter if I flirt a little?"

"I thought you were crazy about Skip."

"He's found prettier girls to walk with."

Millie harrumphed. "I don't trust this man, Stoney. I think he's filled Daddy with a bunch of lies. Obvious to me he's never worked a day on a farm. His skin's too white, and his hands are too smooth. I think he's an opportunist."

"So?"

"Opportunists lie to get what they want."

Didn't seem like a bad idea to me. Honesty never got me anywhere. "I'll do my homework in Uncle Walter's den."

Millie folded her arms across her chest, the way Mama used to do right before she lectured me. "Since when do you do homework?"

I raised my one book in the air. "I decided to turn over a new leaf."

I hated closed places, and Uncle Walter's den was no exception. I tried hard to concentrate on my math. After five minutes, all I could see was Stoney's smile. His scent lingered in the den.

I turned on my uncle's radio and sang along with *Where the Boys Are*. I imagined Stoney kissed me while we walked on the beach. Maybe I could get him to take me to the Grange Dance next month. Uncle Walter wouldn't approve. He said girls shouldn't date until they were sixteen.

Jonas' hollers ended my daydreams. "Supper's ready. I don't want to be late for choir practice. You girls get the table set."

I met Millie in the dining room, and she'd already put the tablecloth on. I wanted to make sure I sat next to Stoney. "I'll set the table tonight. You do it all wrong. I don't want Stoney to think we're ignorant."

Jonas carried in a platter of his famed pot roast covered with potatoes and carrots. "You girls talked with Stoney a long time. Do you think he might want to go to church? Thought I might invite him to mine. Wouldn't hurt Walter to go either."

Millie laughed. "Daddy hates church, though he tolerates you saying grace at the table."

Jonas looked my way. "What about you, Bertie?"

I figured if somebody as kind as Uncle Walter didn't need to go to church, I didn't either. Mama used to drag me to church until not even Papa's horse reins convinced me to go. She finally gave up on me. "Far as I can see, church doesn't make a person good. I know lots of bad people who go to church and lots of good people who don't, like Uncle Walter. Jonas, you're the only good person I know who goes to church."

"Your mother goes to church."

My cheeks heated. "Proves my point."

Jonas shook his head. "True, a church can't save us. God does." He returned to the kitchen, then brought out gravy and homemade applesauce sprinkled with cinnamon. "I don't' go to church to make me a better person. I go to thank the Lord for all my blessings."

I thought about what Jonas said. I didn't see where God had done much for me, though I was grateful for Uncle Walter, Jonas, and Millie. Lately, though, Millie acted more like Mama every day. Besides, God took away my family. Papa died, John went off to Southeast Asia, and Verne took off to who knows where. If God watched over my brothers, I might go to church to say thank you.

I liked the hymns Jonas played on his guitar—my favorite, *Whispering Hope*. I learned the words, and sometimes I sang with Jonas. He said I had a good voice and thought I should join his church choir. When Jonas sang hymns, they comforted me like Papa's hugs.

Stoney sauntered in ahead of Uncle Walter, the scent of Lava soap in his wake. I liked the way he leaned against the archway, a lanky smugness. He'd cross his arms in a way to show off his biceps. "Need help, Jonas?"

Jonas shook his head. "Nope. Might as well sit." He bellowed out the back door. "Walter, get yourself up here. I can't wait on you tonight. Got choir practice and need to leave early."

I showed Stoney where he could sit then plopped down next to him. A few minutes later, Uncle Walter took his usual place at the head of the table, across from Jonas. I set my chair a little closer to Stoney's. Jonas said grace then everyone filled their plates. When

Stoney passed me the platter, I got lost in his big brown eyes, like bowls of dark chocolate ice cream.

Millie straightened and lifted her shoulders. "So, Mr. Rivers—"

"I told you to call me Stoney. Mister is for bankers."

"So, Mr. Rivers, tell us about your work in Idaho—that is if you're really from there."

Uncle Walter slapped the table. "Millie, apologize to our guest."

Stoney smacked his lips. "Ouch, Millie. You're sure direct. No apology necessary, Walter. Truth is, I only picked potatoes for one season."

Millie sat back—she wore smug like some people wore mink.

Stoney set his fork down. "Your father knows I have no dairy experience. I don't intend to make a career as a farmer. I'm an actor."

"Then why do you want to go to New York instead of Los Angeles?"

"I don't really want to be in movies. I'm partial to live theater."

Millie leaned forward. "If you ask me, real theater is Shakespeare. Have you done any Shakespeare, Mr. Rivers?"

I figured Millie would get around to Shakespeare. After she had read *Romeo and Juliet* in ninth grade, she quoted lines every day. I got jealous every time Millie would spout off the balcony scene. General education students didn't study theater of any kind. I had to learn all the good plays on my own. Unless I ran away to New York like Stoney planned to do, I'd never be an actress. Every adult I knew believed Bertie Brown's lot in life was to make babies.

I brightened with the thought. Maybe I could go with Stoney when he left for New York. I wouldn't be any trouble.

Stoney passed me the platter. He squeezed my hand underneath it so no one would see—his intention clear. He stroked my palm like Skip Bilow did when he wanted to sneak out back of the movie theater to smooch.

Millie sneered, her face so red, I thought it might catch on fire. Stoney's squeeze might have fooled Uncle Walter, but it didn't fool Millie for one second. "Bertie, the rest of us would like some pot roast too."

I glanced at Stoney's thick lips. He'd be a great kisser. Skip Bilow was a good kisser but not a great kisser. I let him kiss me all he wanted, though, because I liked that he liked me. Lately, though Skip had taken to kissing Amy Delaney.

How could I let Stoney know I understood what he wanted? Uncle Walter never hit Millie or me, but he did have a temper that would rival a rogue elephant. No telling what he'd do if he knew either one of us kissed boys, especially one Stoney's age.

Somehow I'd find a way. If Stoney liked me, maybe he'd take me to New York with him. I'd let him kiss me even if he turned out to be a bad kisser. A handsome, intelligent man wanted to be with Bertie Brown, the girl with stringy hair who wasn't smart enough to go to college.

Ryan
Christmas Eve
1999

This Stoney character sounded like bad news. How did he manage to fool both Uncle Walter and Jonas? I'd have to wait to find out. After her last sentence, Mom took a deep breath then went back to the counter. She sliced the potatoes like a lumberjack saws a tree.

I didn't have the chance to thank her for her honesty. How hard it must have been to share intimate details with a son. Answers remained hidden; however, I saw my mother in a new light, a troubled teenager who dared to dream.

My father's desertion pained my mother in a way I'll probably never completely understand. Anger at an absent figure surged. Until he left, happiness lived on Maple Street. I wondered what sin I'd committed to make my father leave.

While my mother took to grief like some take to wine, delinquency became my outlet. I teamed up with the Brady boys to knock over old man Grossman's hardware store. Thanks to the verbal lashings of Officer Doty, I learned crime wouldn't get the attention I craved. He managed to get the charges against me dropped if I agreed to informal probation for a few months. If not for his influence, I might have graduated to felonies. I turned my back on the Brady boys, found better friends, kept my grades up, and Officer Doty arranged for part-time work at Belle's. A few months before graduation, I talked with a recruiter.

Some might say I turned my life around in my youth and made good. I suppose some folks applauded how I put my anger aside and cared for my mother. I knew I didn't deserve a single handclap. No power on earth could have made me come back to Granite Falls, except Penny's absolute determination. She argued I needed to come home as much as my mother needed help. She stated her argument with an outstretched finger. "You're as addicted to resentment as your mother is to grief."

As my mother's story slowly unraveled, I no longer felt like the invisible son, and she was no longer a person without a past. She'd been a teenager with thwarted dreams. She'd managed to climb out of a deep pit and deserved to find a different dream to chase. Gina Forbes used to say, "God gives us a new leg when we can't stand on the ones we started with."

I'd long thought Mom should divorce my father. For all we knew, he'd been dead for years. Or worse, he may have started another family somewhere. Mom was still very pretty. She should find a man who'd appreciate her.

Before I could ask Mom to resume her story, R.J. burst into the kitchen, covered from head to feet in crusted snow. "Shut the door. No need to heat the whole outdoors." My loud bark scared even me. I'd craved answers for so long. Now that Mom had finally reached the point of revelation, I worried these distractions would shut the door on her present resolve. I'd go to bed tonight destined to fill in the blank spaces of my life with more fabrications.

"Sorry, Daddy." If he had a tail, he'd have dragged it between his legs. With an eager-to-please temperament, R.J. was an easy child to discipline, obedient as much as a six-year-old knew how to be. I never needed to raise my voice. When I pretended to spank him on his birthday, he saw through my charade. Then we both had a good laugh.

My mother rushed to help R.J. get out of his wet clothes. "You poor child, you're freezing. Would you like hot chocolate?" He wrapped his little arms around his grandmother's neck, and Mom planted a kiss on his cheek.

"Deal. I had lots of fun in the snow."

"I'm glad." Mom said as she heated milk.

R.J. whispered in my ear. "Daddy, you need me to read you a story to calm you down."

Mom handed R.J. his hot chocolate. I rubbed his head so he'd know I wasn't upset with him. "Sounds like a great idea. Take your drink upstairs. I'll be up for the story in a few minutes."

R.J. craned his neck toward the living room. While we let him believe Santa brought the big presents, we always had a few under the tree he knew came from us. "Can I open a present tonight?"

"We'll see," Penny said. "If you eat a good supper."

Most parents want their kids' Christmases to be better than those they had as a child. No challenge for me. After my father abandoned us, my childhood holidays became just another day—no decorations, no presents, and no turkey dinner, the only celebration at the mercy of a kindly neighbor. Even my adult, less-than-enthusiastic participation, proved to be a huge improvement over my boyhood experiences. So, I suppose I had come a long way for R. J.'s sake.

"Deal," he said. R.J. carried his hot chocolate up the steps like an old man, one step at a time, to make sure he didn't spill a drop.

He loved books, so I imagined someday he'd be a writer. I took pride in his intelligence, verified by his teacher. She suggested a move to the gifted class for the following year. If I'd been a peacock, I'd have strut the full length of the hall to know my son was the smartest kid in Granite Falls.

Once R.J. was out of earshot, I turned toward Mom. "I need to go upstairs, but I expect to hear more about this Stoney Rivers when I get back."

Penny shot my mother a secretive glance, proof these two were in cahoots against me. My mother's eyes widened to twice their size. Maybe she thought I'd heard enough for one day. She stuck a fork into the potatoes. "Supper's nearly ready. I won't abide a cold supper that's meant to be hot."

"It's not the end of the world if we delay supper a bit. Besides, it's only four o'clock. Sure could use fresh coffee."

Mom squared her shoulders. "Fine." She took out a tray of Christmas cookies from the freezer. "R.J. will want ice cream with these for his bedtime snack."

When I entered his room, R.J. occupied the middle of the floor, his favorite book of fairy tales opened and ready. "I found a good story to read, Daddy."

I sat on his bed while he acted out the story careful to change his voice to suit each character. Like grandmother like grandson. He could sing, too, a talent, I supposed, he inherited mostly from his mother.

I dreaded the day when my son would reach an age where fathers ceased to be heroes and story time with dad would become a gigantic bore. He stared at the ceiling. "Why didn't the stepmother like Hansel and Gretel? Were they bad?"

"I don't think they were bad children. Maybe the stepmother didn't like them because they weren't her children. Or maybe she felt jealous of them because she thought the father loved his children more than his wife."

"She should still love them even if she didn't grow the babies herself. Denny Hasgood's mother didn't grow him in her belly, but he says his mother loves him just as much as if she did."

"You're right. People don't have to make the baby in order to love it." I wasn't sure if R.J. even knew how a baby was made. Apparently, he knew babies grew inside their mothers.

"Did I grow inside Mommy?"

"Of course."

"Mommy's sad a lot, isn't she?"

"Yes."

"Why is she so sad?"

"I don't know, Sonny. I wish I knew so I could help her not be sad."

"I don't like to see her sad either. I know she loves us. It's okay if she doesn't say it very much. Someday she'll be happy again. We have to be patient."

Gina Forbes used to say, "God gives each child an extra portion of his wisdom." R.J. was the best teacher I ever had. I should trust Penny's love for us as easily as he did.

R.J. finished with a definitive, "The End."

"Thanks for the story."

"Are you calm, now?"

I laughed. "Yeah, I think so."

"I don't like it when you're not calm."

"That makes two of us, Sonny. I will say, though, you're good medicine for me." I kissed the top of his head.

"Maybe you're not calm enough. Do you want another story, to be sure?"

"Maybe later. Right now I need to help Grandma. She expects company tonight."

"She told me. It's her cousin, Millie. They were good friends once upon a time."

"You sure know a lot, don't you?" I pulled R.J. into a hug. As I tousled his hair, I felt grateful he inherited his mother's blonde curls instead of my thin, dark hair. "Up for a game of tiddlywink before bedtime?"

"Deal."

I closed his door then crept down the stairs. I watched Penny frost Millie's cake while Mom gave her step-by-step instructions. I didn't want to intrude on Penny and Mom's moment, the two women more like friends than in-laws. I went back upstairs where R.J. worked with his Lincoln Logs.

"What're you building, Sonny?"

"McDougalville."

"Wow. A whole village? Who's gonna live there?"

"You, Mommy, Grandma, and me, of course. Do you think Grandma's friend would like to live in McDougalville?"

"Maybe."

"I think Mommy won't be sad in my village."

I understood R.J.'s attempt to fix Penny's sadness. I'd have built a city to see my mother smile again. "You'll see, Sonny. Mommy will be herself again, soon." Words I didn't really believe but thought R.J. needed to hear.

Like a cowbell, the aroma of fresh coffee called me back to my mission. Mom was ready to talk.

Bertie
Summer
1961

Uncle Walter believed the first cut of hay, though coarse, was free from contaminants like legumes, alfalfa, and clover. Yet, the first cut often produced quack grass or contained timothy or barley. If the first cut had too many weeds, the cows got sick.

Mama said a girl shouldn't give herself to a man before marriage. Like the first cut of hay, love came with risks. What did Mama know besides hellfire and brimstone? To my ruin, I refused to listen.

Hay season was the busiest time of the year for farmers. Uncle Walter and Stoney spent every bit of daylight to get the hay cut, baled, and stored. They ate supper at a normal hour only on rainy days. I rarely saw Stoney. I remembered how much Papa looked forward to the first cut, usually in spring. Uncle Walter preferred to wait until late June, after he planted, to make the most of longer days and milder weather.

We girls liked to watch Stoney unload the hay onto the elevator while Uncle Walter stacked the bales in the loft. We sat on the fence while they worked. Sweat dripped from Stoney's brow and glistened on his tanned arms. His biceps bulged as he tossed the hay bales. In spite of his strength, he was gentle when we made love.

Uncle Walter signaled to stop the elevator then climbed down. As he wiped his head dry with his red bandana, he came to where Millie and I sat. He looked at us with one eye closed, like a jeweler examines a gem. "I assume both of you will go on to grade eleven?"

I barely passed. My grades were so poor the guidance counselor insisted I attend vocational school, his words repetitively prophetic. "College is not for you, Miss Brown."

I didn't have the heart to disappoint Uncle Walter. "I sent my report card to Mama."

"What about you, Millie?"

She always made the honor roll. Uncle Walter promised he'd buy her a car for graduation if she made honor roll all four years of high. No one would buy Bertie Brown a car because no one expected her to be more than a baby factory. Everyone expected Millie Cooper to become a doctor, a lawyer, or maybe even a politician.

Millie claimed she hated summers. I looked forward to them, especially this year. I'd have more time to spend with Stoney once hay season ended. At least I wouldn't have to hole up in the den every afternoon while Millie studied in her room with her friends. Now I could find excuses to go to the barn to watch Stoney milk.

For the last few weeks, I'd pretended to be a good girl while I lied to Uncle Walter so I could sneak off with Stoney to a private place. When Millie went to her friend's house for a party, I told Uncle Walter I planned to meet up with my own friends at a movie. Jonas understood how neglected I felt since Millie chose her college-bound classmates over me. He dropped me off in front of the theater, so I didn't have to walk into town. I told him I'd find a ride home or call if I didn't. Partly true. Stoney met me in front of the theater as soon as Jonas drove away, then we went off somewhere to make love. We walked back to the house separately so no one would get suspicious.

I understood why we couldn't be together every night. We had to be careful not to get caught. Stoney might lose his job. I looked at my watch. For Uncle Walter, milking time was as sacred a duty as grace at the table for Jonas.

Stoney and Uncle Walter headed to the barn. Millie went to the house to call her friends, and I decided to watch Stoney milk. Maybe we'd steal a kiss behind Uncle Walter's back. He moved down the line of cows, strapping on machines like he'd been born to be a farmer. How quickly he learned.

"You're so fast now, I can't keep up with you." Uncle Walter said. Pride filled me to think Uncle Walter admired the man I loved. I wished I could tell him about Stoney and me. I'd be sixteen in October. When he left for New York, I hoped he'd take me with him.

Uncle Walter tapped me on my shoulder. "Time for you to help Millie set the table. I have an urgent call from Mother Nature. I don't want to see you here when I get back."

When Uncle Walter left, Stoney kissed me on the cheek, I remembered what he'd said the last time we were together. "We have to be real careful no one sees us. You're too young. Some people think what we do is a crime because you're under age. You don't want me in jail, do you?"

I rubbed my cheek where Stoney had kissed me. I wanted more, but I'd have to wait until his next night off. Desire for him clouded my senses. I didn't know how long I could keep our love a secret. Stoney laughed at my stories. I felt smart when I was with him— smarter than Millie. I wanted to shout from a mountaintop that Bertie Brown was loved by the most handsome man in the world.

When we were together, we talked current events. I read the paper every night to keep informed. I watched the nightly news, too. I worried Millie might be suspicious. I told her since John had been sent to Southeast Asia, I tried to keep up with the war news. "Good for you," Millie said.

Stoney knew a lot about the world. "The war in Southeast Asia will only get bigger," he said one night while we cuddled. "It won't be popular. This conflict is all about politics, not concern for an oppressed people. If I get drafted, I'll run off to Canada. I won't fight a war I don't believe in."

What if Stoney got drafted? I didn't want him to fight in the war, but I couldn't stand the thought he might have to defect to Canada. I wanted to marry him, to have his babies. I hoped one of the times we made love I'd get pregnant so he'd have to marry me. Though we saw each other every day, I ached for the nights when we could take short walks. When we couldn't be together, I cried in the hayloft.

I dragged myself away from the barn then went to the house. Millie had set the table without me, all wrong again, worse than ever, as if she wanted me to get mad at her.

I avoided Millie since the first time Stoney and I made love. I was afraid she'd pump me full of questions then find out how we spent time together. Millie had what some people call sixth sense. She could read a person's mind by the way they acted around her. She said psychologists called it *body language* ... how people gave themselves away by what they did more than what they said.

When I saw Jonas wasn't in the kitchen, I turned to go upstairs, but Millie pushed me into a chair.

"Where's Jonas?" I asked.

"He had to go into town to get parts for Daddy's tractor. He'll be back any minute." Millie's eyes blazed with anger. "I saw you two."

"I don't know what you mean." I trembled. Mama always whipped me with Papa's horse reins when she got this angry.

"I saw you kiss Stoney in front of the movie theater last week, and just now in the barn."

"I thought you'd gone to a party with your friends last week?"

"I've been suspicious, so we followed you."

"For your information, he kissed me—on the cheek. We're friends, and sometimes we go for walks. So what?"

Millie pulled me up from the chair then wrestled me against the wall as if she had super-human strength. "I know what a kiss looks like. Doesn't matter who kissed who. Who knows what else you do while you're on a walk."

"It's not a crime to kiss a boy."

"Stoney's not a boy. He's a man."

"Are you gonna rat me out to Uncle Walter?"

She let go of me but stuck a fist near my face. "I should, but I won't. Stoney's a hard worker, and Daddy needs help. If I tell him what you've been up to with Stoney, he'll go into a rage and won't be able to think straight. Besides, I blame you, not Stoney. You're a no good whore, Bertie Brown. I've seen the way you were with Skip Bilow. So I'm not surprised you seduced Stoney too."

I never got upset when Mama called me horrid names. A name can't hurt you unless you believe the name fits. This time, it did. I think my anger reared more at myself than at Millie. "You're jealous because Stoney pays more attention to me than you."

"Stoney Rivers acts like an overgrown teenager. He can go straight to Hades for all I care. If you didn't throw yourself at him, he wouldn't be interested. If you want to sleep with someone, you should find Skip Bilow. He's willing to go all the way with any girl who'll let him."

Millie's meanness hurt more than the worst slap Mama ever gave me. "Maybe it's time I moved back home."

Millie crossed her arms. "Maybe you should call your mother right now."

"What'll you tell Uncle Walter?"

"That you missed your mother and decided to go home."

In some part of my heart, I did miss Mama. I called her from the extension in Uncle Walter's den. I didn't tell her why I wanted to come home. Nor did she ask.

"Of course you can home, Bertie," she said. She didn't say, "I missed you," but the sweetness in her voice made me feel she did. Maybe the argument with Millie was fated so I could make up with Mama.

"Will you come for me right now?"

"I suppose. Don't think you can get out of chores, though."

Within an hour my bags were packed. I left my Elvis cutout behind since I knew Mama would say it wouldn't fit in her car. Since she wouldn't want to step foot in Uncle Walter's house, I waited for her alone on the porch.

I breathed a sigh of relief when I walked into Mama's house.

Could be she only wanted me home to help with housework. Even so, I was glad to be where I was wanted, for whatever reason. Besides, I only had to manage until the New Year. Then I'd go to New York City with Stoney. He'd said, "Bertie, honey, if you give yourself to me, I promise I'll take good care of you." He meant marriage, didn't he?

"You can sleep in your old room," Mama said. "It's my sewing room now, so you can't go to bed until I'm done in there."

There were other rooms Mama could have used for her sewing stuff, but I didn't say anything to her. I didn't want to get into an argument when I'd only been home a few minutes. Didn't matter because Mama went to bed early every night. I'd occupy myself until my room freed up. "We'll manage," I finally squeaked out.

I threw what few stuffed animals I had on the bed then hung my dresses up on the door hooks. Since Mama had stuffed all the bureaus with sewing supplies, I put the rest of my possessions in a box then stuck it under the bed.

Mama and I shared a supper of baloney sandwiches and oranges. "I'm out of milk. I won't have any money until next week. Water will have to do till then." Mama never did seem to have much food in the house.

After we had eaten, Mama went into her sewing room. When the phone rang, she hollered out for me to answer it. I cried a little when I heard Stoney's voice, glad Mama couldn't see my tears.

"Why'd you leave in such a hurry?" Stoney asked. "You didn't even say goodbye."

"I thought maybe I should come home for a little while. I'm sorry I didn't tell you first."

"We'll find a way to be together, Bertie. Don't worry. Probably for the best you moved back in with your mother. Millie acts suspicious. If she told her father, I'd be fired. I need this job until January."

"I love you, Stoney."

"I love you too, Bertie." I thought he meant it. "I'll call again soon then we'll figure out where to meet. Okay?"

Mama came into the room just as I hung up the phone. "Who called?" she asked.

I didn't want to lie. What else could I do? Mama would never understand how much I wanted to be with Stoney. "A friend at school. She wants to meet at the library next week."

She must have believed me since she didn't ask any more questions. "I baked two pies this afternoon. I donated one to the church rummage sale. The other one's in the refrigerator. You can have a piece for your snack if you'd like."

Mama's pie was as good as a hug. She made the best pie in Cold Creek. She'd promised to give me her recipes when I got old enough. When we baked together, love got kneaded into the dough. "I'll help myself. I suppose it's your bedtime now."

Mama looked at her watch. "Clean sheets are in the hall closet. Goodnight, Bertie."

"Goodnight, Mama."

We hadn't spoken much. Yet, the few words we exchanged made me feel hopeful we might actually get along. A least until I turned sixteen.

I made up my bed then washed up for the night. The woman who stared back at me in the mirror seemed a stranger. She was no longer the girl who left Mama's last year. How could I have changed so much in so short a time? I took the stuffed animals off my bed then stored them in the attic.

As I changed into a nightgown, I imagined I lay next to Stoney in the meadow not far from the farm, the last place we made love. Then I remembered Millie. I think I shed more tears to be separated from her than Stoney. I had missed her company. We'd been so close before she found new friends. I missed our dances down the steps and our fights over Elvis as we listened to his records. I missed our pillow fights too. Mama preached the Good Book said to put away childish things. "You're a grown woman now, Bertie Brown," I told myself. "Time to act like one."

Even though Mama gave me plenty of work to do, summer dragged on like a sermon. Mama's chores made no sense at all. One time, she asked me to paint the fence when I'd painted it only a week before. Every day I scrubbed the house and weeded the garden. I did whatever she asked me to do whether I agreed it needed to be done or not as long as I could be free on Friday nights to see Stoney.

As far as Mama knew, I went into town to meet my friends at the movies. Either Mama didn't care, or she'd become easy to fool. Though we lived five miles from town, she never asked what I did for a ride. She never waited up for me, either.

Truth was, I'd walk two miles through the woods to meet Stoney at the Davidson cabin. After Papa's death, Mama had sold most of the property to the Davidsons, and they hired her to look after the place when they moved to California. I snuck Mama's key so I could meet Stoney there.

He told me I shouldn't walk home in the dark without a flashlight. I didn't need one. I knew every rut in the path from Mama's house to the cabin. Once I forgot to bring a flashlight, and Stoney stormed off. I made sure not to forget again. I thought he had to love me a lot to be so worried about my safety.

August brought an early chill. By the time Labor Day weekend arrived, the trees glowed with autumn colors. Stoney had the whole day off. I looked forward to our date since I hadn't seen him in a few weeks. When he had to cancel, I cried for two days, though I understood how emergencies creep up fairly often on a farm.

I put away the last dish, grabbed the flashlight from my dresser and headed out the door. The shorter days cast shadows like specters ready to gobble their prey. I sat on the picnic bench while I waited for Stoney. The sound of tires on gravel made me turn around, fearful Mama had come to the cabin, or someone reported a break-in to the police. I gasped when I saw Jonas' truck, until Stoney got out, leaned against it then pulled his cap so it nearly hid his eyes.

"Why did you take Jonas' truck? You always walk here."

"I can't stay long, Bertie. Jonas thinks I borrowed his truck to make a quick run into town to pick up feed."

By now, Stoney would have pulled me in for a kiss, taken my hand then walked to the cabin. With a sigh, he twisted his cap around then crossed his arms. "Bertie, we have to talk."

My stomach flip-flopped.

"I'm gonna say this right off."

My back stiffened as I looked into icy eyes.

"I can't see you anymore, Bertie."

My ears rang from the rush of hot blood. "Why not?"

"Too many people are suspicious. Yesterday, Jonas asked me where I go every Friday night. If they find out about us, I'll be fired or worse."

"Worse?"

"I told you. I'd go to jail. You're too young."

"I'm not too young to make you happy."

He smiled a little. "You do make me happy, Bertie. But, we can't see each other anymore."

"What about your promise? You said a promise is a promise."

"What promise?"

"You promised to take care of me."

"An expression, Bertie. What did you think I meant?"

"We'd get married, and you'd take me to New York City."

As I glanced toward the pond, a big bass jumped out of the water as if to say, "How foolish to think someone actually loved you." My eyes misted. No way will I let Stoney see me cry. I forced the tears back. If need be, I'd dam them up forever.

"Be reasonable, Bertie. I can't marry anyone right now, and I certainly don't want to drag a country girl to the city. You'd be hurt. I'd get the blame. You're a sweet girl. I loved being with you. Sadly, good things eventually end."

"Well, for your information, Stoney Rivers, I wouldn't marry you now if you were the last man on earth. So you go ride out of here like the jerk you are."

Not very clever. I shook too much to be clever.

Millie told people off with style. Stoney broke my heart, and I wanted him to bleed. My words wouldn't have cut a piece of paper.

He turned in silence, got into the truck and drove out of my life. I waited for the avalanche of tears, but they never came. I threw my flashlight into the pond. Maybe a wild animal would attack me in the dark and end my misery. Unfortunately, nature didn't cooperate. When I got back to the house, I knew I'd have to find a way to live without Stoney Rivers.

I hoped beyond hope Mama might still be up. I tapped on her door, but she yelled at me to leave her alone so she could go to sleep. I stared at the ceiling. I don't think I slept at all. In fact, I had no memory of the next three days until Mama banged the door so hard I thought she'd break it down.

"Bertie Brown, you best be off to school before they send the truant officer for you. If he comes out here, you can be sure I'll give you double what the law gives you."

Mama's tantrums had long ago lost the power to frighten me. If she came at me with Papa's horse reins, I'd take whatever punishment she doled out. The last time she gave me welts, I ran away to Uncle Walter's. Millie hugged me, her words a melody of comfort. "Millie, I'm tired of being beaten like a disobedient mule," I said. "I'm never going back again. I thought I'd die this time. I didn't, though. Do you suppose God keeps me alive because he hates me?"

Millie shook my shoulders as if to make a point. "God doesn't hate you. Jonas believes God doesn't let us suffer without a reason. I think life is a gift. Like all gifts, we should appreciate both the good and the bad, make the most of the time we have." Until the day we fought over Stoney, Millie always knew what to say to make me feel better.

I missed Millie. I wanted my friend to hug me now. To reassure me God didn't hate me. A new school year loomed. I'd hoped this year would be different. I'd work hard on my grades and prove to the world how smart I really was. I didn't want to go to school with a bunch of red marks, and I'd already missed one whole day. "I'm up, Mama. You don't need to get Papa's horse reins."

I put on the dress Uncle Walter bought me for the Grange Dance last May—a white sleeveless rayon with a multi-colored belt. Stoney said I looked a little like a movie star. If Skip Bilow saw me in it, maybe he'd like me again. Didn't matter. I decided I was done with the male gender, unless by some miracle, I met someone like Uncle Walter, Jonas, or Papa, the only good people I'd ever known, besides Millie. *More than likely*, I told myself, *the world of men is populated with the likes of Stoney Rivers.*

Ryan
Christmas Eve
1999

I blew a breath of disbelief. Since I'd returned to Granite Falls, my mother slowly emerged from a self-made cocoon to dwell among the purposed. Then again, she never spoke much more than what was necessary to get a meal together or take care of R.J. When I was a boy, she certainly never talked about sex. My education came from Harvey Forbes, Gina's husband. He handed me a box of condoms and said, "Don't get a girl pregnant unless you intend to marry her."

A week later, I overheard Gina's conversation with my mother, more one-sided as were all their talks. She'd brought over a marble cake and stayed to have tea with my mother. Gina clicked a story about a girl in my chemistry class. "Do you remember Candy Mayville?" Gina asked.

Mom nodded. "The girl Lenny Gerrard got pregnant then deserted?"

"Not so much deserted. Lenny's parents paid Candy to give the baby up for adoption. I heard yesterday, she lost the baby."

Mom's eyes had grown twice their normal size. "Just judgment." She picked up the dishes then washed them in the sink, probably the most she'd moved all day. At that time, I thought Mom's response had been hard-hearted. Maybe Candy shouldn't have let herself get pregnant. Still, a baby died. Seemed compassion should have taken precedence over condemnation at a time like that

I reexamined those words in light of what Mom had just told me. What had caused my mother to be as harsh a judge as Grandma

Brown? I supposed life had hit her once too often—even before she met my father—harder punches than an abusive mother, a jerk of a boyfriend, or the loss of a good friend. Of course, these had made life difficult. Yet, none of these disappointments explained why my mother's heart turned to stone after my father left.

Mom wiped her eyes then glanced at the clock. "Good grief, I'm way behind schedule. Penny, start the corn. I'll set the table to make sure it's done right. Potatoes need to be mashed, and there's gravy to be made. I did the gelatin earlier so it should be set by now. Ryan, get R.J. Make sure he washes his hands. You men don't ever wash your hands after your nature calls. Don't want unwashed hands at my table …"

Mom spewed words like a scared person had to turn on all the lights as if the sound of her own voice could stop the flood of dark memory. Maybe I shouldn't have pushed her so hard to remember. Not likely she'd tell me more with R.J.'s little ears around. We tried hard to child-proof our language around R.J., who didn't miss a word uttered in his presence and could repeat television shows verbatim.

I paused to watch my son at play. He set a green Lincoln Log roof on top of a cabin. I smiled with pride at R.J.'s ingenuity. His village, complete with a bank, store, hospital, gas station, school, fire house, and residential homes, was constructed from an assortment of building blocks and toys. He'd placed figurines of all sizes and shapes hither and yon within his make-believe town.

"Wow! That's quite a village you got there, Sonny."

"Everybody is happy in McDougalville. See." He picked up a Little People man dressed in work clothes similar to the Dickies I wore to the factory. "This is you, Daddy. You are on your way to see Aunt Belle. She lives in the village, too."

"Hungry?"

"I think I could eat a whole turkey all by myself. But I'll share it."

"Good. Supper's ready if you are."

"Do I get to open a present after we eat?"

"If your mother says so. Now go wash your hands."

I heard running water but made sure he'd used soap as Mom asked. She'd sniff his hands to be certain and blame me if she didn't smell soap.

We raced downstairs. I held back slightly to make sure R.J. won the race.

"You're a rotten egg, Daddy."

My eyes caught site of Penny as she put a bowl heaped high with mashed potatoes on the table. "I'm a rotten something all right. Let's sit."

Penny's glare confused me—a half come hither look she used to give me when she wanted to make love and half annoyed like when I forgot to pick milk up on the way home from work. Sometimes Penny's facial clues were harder to solve than a thousand-piece puzzle.

Mom had folded the autumn colored napkins to look like little turkeys. R.J. made gobble sounds as he picked up his and spread it across his lap as if to the manor born. I'd never understood my mother's fascination with how a table looked until our recent talk. I think now I get it. She wants her table to be an invitation. I promised myself to never make fun of her peculiarities again.

Mom handed me the carving knife. She knew full well I'd make a mess of the bird. I hacked off two pieces of white meat before Mom took the knife away. She lit the centerpiece candles then sat on her usual chair next to Penny across from me.

I chanced a smile for my wife. No response. Not that I expected one. What few smiles she shared those days only went to R.J.

"Normally we dig in," Mom said. "Since its Christmas Eve, maybe we should say grace."

"You're right, of course, Bertie," Penny said. "R.J. should learn to say grace at the table."

"Do you plan to start a new tradition?" I asked. Until that night, prayers had never been said at our Maple Street home. Gina Forbes threw around God's name like he was a special friend of hers. "The Lord," this or "The Lord," that. I might have prayed once or twice to ask God to help me find my father. Since he never returned, I figured if their God existed, he didn't care about our family.

I folded my hands together like I'd seen people pray in movies. "Go ahead, Mom, if you want to."

"I've only attended church for a few months. But, I think the head of the house should say grace. That's you, Ryan."

I glanced at my wife. "Penny went to Sunday school. I think she's probably the most qualified at this table."

Penny bit her lower lip. "Here's one R.J. could learn. God is great. God is good. And we thank Him for this food. Amen."

I nodded approval. "Go ahead, say it, Sonny."

"God is good. The food is good. Amen!"

"Close enough, I guess."

"Daddy, who's Grace and why do we have to thank her for the food Grandma made?"

I rendered a nervous cackle because once more, I'd have to give R.J. an answer to a subject I knew nothing about. I dove into my pool of ignorance. "Grace isn't a person. It's a term used when people tell God thank you for their food."

Mom offered a half smile. "Pretty good explanation, Ryan."

R.J. scrunched his face into a portrait of concern. "Grandma says God is everywhere, and he knows everything. Makes no sense why we have to tell him stuff he already knows."

Penny met my gaze. For the first time in a year, laughter shone in those big blues as if she couldn't wait to hear what idiotic answer I'd give our son.

"I won't fib, Sonny. God's a mystery to me."

I shot my mother an accusatory glance. "Sounds like you and R.J. have had some religious conversations. I think this is more in your ballpark than mine."

Mom squared her shoulders. "R.J. asked *you*, not me."

I passed the ball right over to Penny. "Your mother's the Bible scholar, Sonny. Ask her."

Penny smiled as she lifted R.J.'s head. "What Grandma says is true. God knows everything because he is everywhere. He's a spirit. He also wants to come into our hearts and be our friend."

R.J. glanced at the ceiling. "Wow. God must be bigger than this whole house if he's everywhere."

"Yes. He's big, and he's powerful."

R.J. tried to balance his fork on his plate and laughed when it plopped against his glass. "If God's so big, how can he live inside a heart?"

Penny plowed straight on. "God lives inside us when we ask Jesus into our hearts."

"Grandma says Jesus is why we have Christmas. It's *his* birthday. He was God's son."

"Jesus lived on earth a long time ago. He is in heaven with God now. If we ask Jesus into our hearts, he helps us know God like he knows God. We have to ask him to come into our hearts. He doesn't force his way. He's very polite."

R.J. took a big bite of turkey. "Did you ask Jesus into your heart, Mommy?"

Penny's eyes misted. "A long time ago."

"Is he still there?"

"I'm not sure. I've been mad at God for a very long time."

R.J. took a sip of water then gulped town his turkey while he poked a finger at Penny's chest. "I think if God is *so* big and Jesus is like God, then if you asked him into your heart, he's not afraid that you're mad at him. I expect he's still in there. You just forgot to look for him."

Gina Forbes used to say we could never understand God until we learned to think about him like a child. As for me, the whole God-came-to-earth-in-the-form-of-Baby-Jesus dogma seemed too complicated. Belle Thompson tried to explain the Godhead, three-in-one concept. It boggled my mind. R.J.'s interpretation made sense.

He shoveled two more bites of turkey. "I'm finished with my supper. Can I open my present now?"

I looked at the food still left on his plate. "What about the rest?"

He shook himself to express frustration, then stuffed his mouth until his cheeks ballooned like a squirrel's.

"Easy, Sonny. You'll choke."

He managed to eat the rest of his food in under two minutes, then he raised his hands in the air and swiveled in his chair. "All done!"

Penny looked toward the den. "If you go into my room, you might find a present there."

R.J. burst from the table at top speed. I heard his squeals of joy before any of us could catch up to him. "Oh, boy, a toboggan. Can I try it out on the hill at the end of the street?"

"Sure. I'll take you. Go get your gear on."

He squatted. "Mark, get set, go." He bumped into Mom and Penny as they came out of the kitchen.

"I got a toboggan. Daddy's gonna take me to the hill to try it out." He ran into the kitchen to put on his snowsuit.

I followed, but Mom grabbed my arm. "Just a minute, Ryan. I want you to know I made up my mind. You do need to hear the rest of what I got to say. It hurt me to tell you about Stoney. I think now I understand how important it is for you to know your father didn't leave because of you. He loved you. I'm the one to blame."

"I'm glad you told me about Stoney. But you shouldn't feel ashamed of what happened. Stoney had no business having relations with you."

"Even though I wanted him to?"

"A fifteen-year-old can't even decide what shoes to wear to school let alone wise up to a creep like Stoney. As for Pop? No one forced him to walk out on people who loved him." I wanted to believe what I had just said to my mother, yet I wondered. What could my mother have done to make her husband walk away?

I put on my fleece-lined jacket, then waited outside while Mom helped R.J. into his snowsuit. The cold felt like a thousand prickly needles, and I soon wished I'd taken the time to put on a pair of gloves. Too lazy to go back inside, I shoved my hands in my pants pocket and wrapped my fingers around the photograph I'd found earlier. I intended to ask Penny about it when I came back to the house.

I thought about R.J.'s triangular vision of God. I supposed the universe had been formed by an intelligent being. When I looked at all the evil in the world, I questioned if the Creator still cared about what he had made. Grandma Brown's version of God sounded harsh. I liked Penny's idea, the best of all the theories I'd ever heard. Her earlier explanation to R.J. lined up with things Belle Thompson said.

I wished this God of theirs would help my family. Help me know why a pretty girl like Millie ran away from people who cared about her, why a good man like my father disappeared, and why my beautiful wife no longer loved me. If he could at the very least help me understand these mysteries, I might want to believe in him.

R.J. came out from the kitchen, his toboggan in tow.

We slid until I couldn't feel my face anymore. "Time we went in, Sonny."

I ran my hands under hot water while R.J. got out of his snowsuit. "Get into your pajamas. I'll bring your treat to your room."

"Can I stay up to see Grandma's friend?"

"No. Millie won't be here until much later."

I hurried down the steps in hopes Mom was ready to talk again. At the moment, she was too busy preparing R.J.'s snack. I understood a little better why she doted on the boy. I sat at the table next to Penny. Wonder of wonders, she didn't move to the other side.

"What time do you think Millie will get here?" I asked.

"Not sure exactly. I hope she doesn't get lost in the dark."

"Mom, sit down. R.J.'s cookies can wait a few minutes. You said you wanted to explain what happened to Millie. Now's as good a time as any."

She leaned against the counter, a block of resistance. She'd need a prod or two. "Did you ever run into Millie at school?"

An innocent enough question.

Mom covered her face as she sighed. After a brief hesitation, she said, "Yes, Ryan. To my damnation, I did."

Bertie
December
1961

A prolonged sadness settled over me after Stoney and I broke up. Though I attended school faithfully, I couldn't concentrate and yawned through most of my classes, except English. Mr. Morton thought even vocational students should be well read. I enjoyed most of the assignments, though the books were what he called classics.

My sixteenth birthday came and went with no celebration as I'd hoped, only a card from Mama. If she would have let me have a party, I'd have invited Millie even if she said she wouldn't come. I missed her so.

Nights bored me more than school. Mama made me turn off television when she went to bed. I'd lie on the sofa and stare until the moon rose too high for me to see.

As Christmas neared, I wondered if Mama would do anything special. Sometimes she did. Other times she hollered at everyone's decorations and said, "It's our Savior's birthday. We should give him presents instead of buying them for ourselves."

The kids at school buzzed with excitement over their Christmas plans. As the holiday neared, Mama surprised me. "Would you like to cook a nice dinner for Christmas?"

"Oh, could we, Mama?"

She handed me a twenty-dollar bill for groceries. "Buy whatever you'd like."

Though I knew I'd fix a special dinner for Mama and me, I still wished I could be at Uncle Walter's for Christmas Eve. Jonas always had a big birthday for Millie. She'd be sixteen soon. Likely Uncle Walter would make her party an extra special occasion.

Once in a great while, I'd see Millie in the hall. She never took the time to stop—always in a hurry. The college preparatory classes were on the third floor so she rarely came to the vocational wing, and I had no reason to be with the smart kids either.

I also missed Stoney—missed the way he played with my hair and told corny jokes. I wished he'd call if only to see how I was. He didn't have to apologize. If he did call, I'd pretend to be a little mad then let him convince me to meet him at the Davidson cabin. I still wished he would take me to New York City with him. He didn't have to marry me or even be my boyfriend.

My teacher towered over me. "Miss Brown, care to tell the class what seems to be more important than conjugating sentences?"

My classmates laughed while my cheeks burned. "I'm sorry, Mr. Morton, I didn't pay attention. I won't let it happen again."

Only, it did happen, again and again.

Sometimes, I'd go to the library after school to read newspapers since Mama didn't want to spend the money to have one delivered to the house. I read where Uncle Walter's friend, Peter Hannigan, died. I asked Mama if we could go to the funeral. She thought a minute. "I don't think so, Bertie. I liked the man, but I never got along with Walter. I suspect since you waltzed right out of your uncle's house without a word to him, you had your problems with him too. I don't think we'd be welcomed."

I wanted to explain that I left Uncle Walter's because of Millie, not him. If I told the truth, she'd ask what we fought about. I couldn't tell her about Stoney. Mama would likely throw me out on the street.

When the bell rang, I hurried to pick up my Business Math textbook, my next class before I spent the afternoon in horticulture studies.

I was surprised to see Millie waiting by my locker. When I came up to her, she placed an invitation in my hand. "I don't blame you if you don't want to come. I treated you so badly. I'm sorry I made you leave. I miss you. The invitation is for my sweet sixteen birthday party. It wouldn't be the same if my best friend in the whole world isn't there. Please say you'll come."

I thought I might refuse even though my heart jumped at the chance to see Stoney again. I noticed Millie's sunken eyes. Her sweater hung to her knees. "You look real pale, Millie. Are you sick?"

"No. So will you come?"

"Yeah. Maybe Mama will bring me over."

I wanted to ask Millie if Stoney had left for New York City. Instead, I asked after Jonas and Uncle Walter.

"Everybody's fine. We all miss you."

Stoney too?

The bell rang for the next class. We'd both be late. "I'll see you at your party, Millie."

I managed to sneak into the room seconds before my teacher took attendance. All I could think about was Millie's party. Would Stoney be there? If he did come, I'd pretend I didn't care. I didn't want to spoil Millie's special day.

Mama said she'd give me a ride, and she'd be sure to pick me up before nine o'clock so she could get home before her bedtime. I bought Millie a paisley scarf and gold leaf pin with money Mama gave me for all the work I did at the Davidson cabin. I knew what she paid me was less than what Mr. Davidson sent her. I didn't mind. When I cleaned the cabin, I remembered the special times I'd spent there with Stoney.

I spent all Christmas Eve day getting ready for the party. I wore a taffeta dress I'd bought at the second-hand store. When I arrived at Uncle Walter's, Jonas pulled me into a big hug. "Here's our Bertie! My, we've missed you around here." Jonas winked. "Don't tell Walter, but I missed the records, too—especially Elvis. Although, Millie didn't like to play them very often. She preferred classical."

Mama didn't have a phonograph—no matter since I didn't own any records.

Millie sat on the couch with her friends. I almost asked Jonas if I could call Mama to come get me. Why did they have to be there?

Millie has a right to invite anyone she wants, I scolded myself. Besides, she said I was her best friend in the whole world. So what did it matter if she sat with her other friends?

Millie jumped off the couch and threw her arms around my neck. "I'm so glad you came." She shooed her friends away and told me to sit next to her. "Stoney will be in later," she said. "He finished up the chores on his own so Daddy could be here for the party."

A tingle like sipping a milkshake rushed up my spine to think I'd see Stoney again.

When I gave Millie her present, she put the scarf and pin right on. "I love them, Bertie. This pin and scarf will always be my favorites." They looked pretty against her white sweater. She pulled me up from the couch and dragged me to the Christmas tree. Jonas took a bunch of pictures with his new Polaroid, then Millie handed each girl a photo of her by the tree. On mine, she wrote: *To my best friend. So we'll always remember.*

Jonas went into the kitchen then returned with a tray of cookies. He served each guest a glass of punch then signaled for a toast. "To the birthday girl."

We played Charades, and I was glad Millie had chosen me for her team. We won. "That's because you're such a good actress, Bertie," she said.

After the games, Jonas played his guitar while we sang Christmas carols. Everyone squealed with delight when Jonas brought out the birthday cake, edged with green and gold leaves and a big red **16** in the middle. He lit the candles then sang "Happy Birthday." Millie made a wish then blew out all the candles on the first try.

"You can't tell anyone what you wished for, Millie, or it won't come true," I said.

Uncle Walter rose. "A cake this pretty deserves a special cake server, don't you think, Jonas?"

He nodded.

"Don't cut the cake yet, Millie. I'll be right back. I have a surprise for you." Uncle Walter stepped into the study and returned with a big cedar chest in tow. "This is your hope chest, Millie. Before your mother died, she made me promise to make you one for your sixteenth birthday." He handed Millie a white rectangular box. "This is your mother's cake server, the one handed down to her from her mother. I hope someday you'll have a daughter of your own to pass it on to."

Her eyes filled with tears while we all waited for her speech. I thought maybe she was sad because her mother didn't live to give it to Millie herself. With no explanation, Millie threw the cake server onto the coffee table then ran upstairs. Silence followed as the rest of us glanced from person to person, not sure what we should do. Go after her or wait until she came back down.

A car honked. "That's our ride," Veronica said. "We should probably go. Tell Millie we had a good time."

Jonas wrapped two cake slices in aluminum foil then gave one to each of Millie's friends. "Take these with you." He walked Mary and Veronica to the door. I overheard him say, "I'm sure Millie will be fine. I'll have her call you tomorrow."

Uncle Walter turned to face me. "Bertie, why don't you talk to Millie? Maybe it's her time of the month."

I went upstairs, trepidation with each step. Whatever bothered Millie had to be more serious than her period. I went right in without knocking. Millie sat on her bed, her knees drawn to her chest.

"What's wrong?"

She bit her lip.

"You can tell me. I'm your best friend. You said so yourself." I slid the vanity stool next to the bed then sat.

Millie swung her feet over the side. "If I tell you, will you promise not to say a word to Jonas or my father?"

"I can't make a promise until I know what it is."

She squeezed a white Teddy Bear to her chest. "Bertie, I'm pregnant."

I didn't believe her. Millie didn't even have a boyfriend last I knew. "Is that supposed to be funny?"

"I wish it were a joke. It's not. I'm serious. I saw Doc Johnson a few days ago. He confirmed what I suspected. He said he'd give me a week to tell Daddy, or he'd tell him himself. Oh, Bertie, I'm so afraid to tell my father. If he doesn't kill me, he'll be so disappointed in me I'll want to kill myself."

Millie wasn't the only pregnant teenager in Cold Creek. Every year girls disappeared for months at a time, rumored they went off someplace to have a baby. Millie could have her baby, give it away to be adopted, come back home, and no one need know the truth. She could still go to college. I didn't see it as much a tragedy as a major interruption. "I'm surprised. You always said you weren't interested in boys right now. When did you change your mind? Who's the father? Is it Skip Bilow?"

"No, it's not Skip. I don't want to say until I tell the father. He has a right to know. After I tell him, then together we'll tell Daddy."

"You can tell me, though, right?"

"I'm afraid you'll be mad."

"I never should have gone away, Millie. Maybe if I'd stayed, I could have stopped you before you got so serious with a boy. I know how not to get pregnant."

"I thought I knew, too. Guess I didn't know as much as I thought I did."

"Do you love the father?"

"No. Not really. I can't explain what happened. We had a fight, and before I knew what happened, we made love. We only did it a few times."

I scowled. "Any farm girl knows it only takes once. So who's the father?"

Millie threw the Teddy Bear to the floor. "Stoney Rivers."

I wished I'd been a true friend to Millie. Instead, I let rage blind me. The cold truth hit me like thousands of ice particles. Millie hadn't asked me to leave because she thought I'd acted like a shameless hussy. She wanted Stoney to herself, and now she was pregnant by the man I loved—she would have the baby with him I wanted to make.

A sickness I couldn't name grabbed my stomach. I swallowed the urge to throw up. I knew I acted selfishly, yet, I couldn't stop the anger. My friend was in trouble, but I hated her for being with Stoney. They both betrayed me. Even then, to my self-loathing, I knew if Stoney asked me to go to New York City with him, I'd go; and I would never look back in regret.

If Uncle Walter knew, he'd be so mad he'd make Stoney leave. Then he'd probably send Millie away to a special home. I was sixteen now so I could go away with Stoney. Why stay in this horrible town any longer?

Millie grabbed my arm. "Bertie, the look on your face—it scares me—as if you wish I were dead."

Did I wish her dead? Of course not, but I did want to turn back the clock to a time hate did not consume me.

I ran to the door. "I'm telling Uncle Walter."

"No, Bertie. Oh, please, no!"

I tuned out Millie's pleas as I bounded down the stairs. Uncle Walter and Jonas sat on the couch, worried looks on their faces. Though out of breath, I still managed to blurt out the words destined to damn everyone who heard them. "Millie's pregnant. Stoney Rivers is the father."

MIRACLE ON MAPLE STREET

Ryan
Christmas Eve
1999

So Millie ran away because she was afraid when her father found out about her pregnancy. Made sense. Only, why did Mom feel she'd damned Uncle Walter and Jonas because she told them about Millie? Maybe Uncle Walter sent Millie to a place for unwed mothers, and she decided not to come back home. Or Stoney might have come through and manned up to his responsibility to Millie and the baby. Though, in my book, she was better off without him.

Impatience whirled. Why did my mother feel compelled to tell me about her life as a teenager? As sad as those years were, how did these experiences explain why my father left? Or Millie's connection to his disappearance?

R.J. came downstairs, his pajamas on backward, his face downcast. "Daddy, did you forget about my snack?"

Mom hurried to the freezer. "How about I give you an extra scoop of ice cream and two extra cookies because you had to wait for such a long time?"

"Deal!"

When his improved plate was ready, I handed it to him. "Go on. Take your dessert to your room. I owe you a game of tiddlywink, remember?"

"I didn't forget, but I thought you did."

"No, I didn't. I'll be up in a minute or two."

"Deal." R.J. walked at a snail's pace. I waited for him to reach the top before I started up. He shouted back to me, "See, I'm real careful."

Mom joined me at the foot of the steps. "I can tell you're confused as to what my argument with Millie has to do with your father. I'll explain soon. First, go spend time with R.J."

"I take it Uncle Walter didn't react well to the news. I'm not surprised. If I had a daughter, I'd want to kill the guy."

Mom shivered.

"Are you cold? Do you want me to turn up the furnace?"

"I'm fine. If I'd known what would happen next, I'd have kept my mouth shut. Ryan, I never held it against your father for leaving us."

The way Mom put those two sentences together made me more convinced than ever Millie's disappearance and Pop's desertion were connected, like opposite ends of a chain. Anger flared. "I don't get it. Pop's leaving hurt you bad. Or don't you remember how you were afterward?"

She stepped back. "I'm sorry my grief caused you pain. We, your father and I, are the ones who failed you, not the other way around. I don't expect you to forgive either one of us. I only want you to understand what happened."

"Why? He won't ever be back."

"I always believed he would … someday. Maybe that's why I stared out the window so much. I hoped against hope before I finally started to heal. When you brought Penny and R.J. home, I found a reason to live again. Then yesterday, I got the letter from Millie. Maybe God's been at work right along."

"Well, Mom, they say Christmas is a time for miracles. Maybe Millie's coming to see you after all these years is *your* Christmas miracle. If anyone deserves one, you do."

She kissed me on the cheek. A mother's love is a treasure—one I thought I'd lost a long time ago—and now found again on Christmas Eve. Maybe this was *my* Christmas miracle.

Mom pointed upstairs. "Go."

I preferred to let her finish what she started, but R.J.'s impatient hail echoed through the house. "Daddy! How long will you be?"

"Be right up, Sonny." I turned to my mother. "Mom, whatever happened between you and Pop ... I won't blame you. Life sometimes throws things at us beyond our ability to control."

A loud crash reverberated from the kitchen. We both rushed in. Penny stood over a broken dish, her face drooped and ashen. Mom hauled out a broom. "Don't worry. It's only a plate."

"What's wrong? Are you sick?" I asked.

"No. Go on up to R.J."

Should I go when Penny seemed so scared? Mom gestured toward the steps as R.J.'s impatient howl wafted on the air. "Come on, Daddy. I got the game all set up."

As I climbed the first few steps, I overheard the conversation in the kitchen.

"Bertie, it's time you forgive yourself for what happened. Like Ryan said, we can't control every aspect of our lives."

"Physician, heal thyself," Mom said.

I'd heard Gina Forbes say those words to my mother from time to time. I never really knew what she meant by them, but I knew beyond any doubt Mom and Penny had shared their secrets with one another. For whatever reason, neither felt comfortable to let me in on them. Mom had begun to talk about hers. I hoped Penny would before the night was over.

Should I go back downstairs? R.J.s persistent calls pulled me toward him. "I got the yellow, Daddy."

I followed R.J. to his room; his pajamas were smeared with chocolate ice cream.

I stretched out on the floor, propped up on one elbow while R.J. sat cross-legged. He liked to be in charge whenever we played a game. Most of a six-year-old's world towered above his reach. Naturally, a kid would want to control whatever he could. "Here are your red winks. Now line them up in a row, like mine."

I deliberately messed up the order—a tease so I could hear his infectious laugh.

He giggled on cue then pointed out the error of my ways as he reset the winks with precision, like Mom's dinnerware. "No, Daddy. See? The two big ones go like this. The four small ones go there."

We squidged off. My wink landed only two inches from my baseline. R.J.'s landed in the pot.

After fifteen minutes, I had yet to pot a wink, and R.J. had potted all of his. "Squopped you, Daddy!"

"Maybe I should enter you in a tournament."

"What's a tournament?"

"Never mind." I wet a towel down, washed his hands and face, and cleaned up the smudge on his pajamas. "Time for lights out." I helped him put the game away and tucked him into bed. "Go to sleep, so Santa Claus can come."

"Deal." He stared at the ceiling, ready to pop another deep question. Turned out it wasn't a question, rather he made a wish. "Sure would be nice if we could have another special day like this."

Shame filled me. I'd been away so much R.J. thought our time together had been special. Guilt riddled all justification. I'd spent far too much time away from my family. After work, I headed to Belle's looking for peace of mind. Trouble was, I couldn't escape the turmoil inside of me. So I headed out for booze and guzzled a few at various bars until I gathered enough courage to face Penny's rejection. Most nights, I ate supper by myself after R.J. had gone to bed. Maybe I hadn't moved out of the house, but perhaps I had so distanced myself from my family, my son felt emotionally abandoned. Time spent with your child should never be labeled a special day. "Tomorrow's Christmas. That'll be special."

I turned off his light, then went back downstairs. Mom and Penny had set up the card table in the den to wrap R.J.'s presents. I picked up a miniature black pickup truck. "This looks exactly like *The Beast*."

I'd bought the truck off a rancher in Georgia while stationed at Fort Benning. The first vehicle I'd ever owned. When Penny got into it, she smiled, as if she understood how a man feels about his ride. "So, how long have you had this beast?"

The name stuck.

Call me sentimental. I'd been offered good money for the truck. As far as I was concerned, *The Beast* would never be for sale—both it and Penny, my first and only loves.

Penny glanced up at me. "I thought R.J. would like it."

I wanted to scoop her up, take her to my room right then. Unfortunately, the glimmer of hope disappeared with my first step toward her. I sensed my wife fought a war. As a soldier, I understood not every battle ended in victory.

I poured myself a glass of milk. Mom came into the kitchen behind me. As she sat, she met my gaze. "I'm ready, now. Are you?"

MIRACLE ON MAPLE STREET

Bertie
Christmas
1961

I wish I could forget what happened next. Like scum, bad memories rise to the surface. They devour you one maggot at a time.

If Millie had waited a few minutes, or if Stoney had stayed in the barn, Jonas might have helped Uncle Walter calm down. Life isn't scripted like a movie scene where characters take turns when they act their parts so you're clear on who said what when. Instead, the rest happened all at once, like a three-ringed circus show.

Uncle Walter smashed his fist into the glass gun cabinet, pulled out his shotgun, loaded it, and slung it over his shoulders. "I'm going to kill that—"

Jonas shouted at Uncle Walter. "Put the rifle away. You won't shoot anybody. That's not the way to help Millie. We'll wait here until she comes back downstairs then discuss it like civilized people."

Stoney waltzed into the house and whistled the first line to *Happy Birthday*—he stopped cold when he saw Uncle Walter with a raised shotgun.

Millie rushed down the steps as Uncle Walter pulled back the trigger. She pushed the barrel up, and the rifle went off, the echo like dynamite to my ears. A trickle of blood seeped down Stoney's cheek where the bullet must have grazed him. He didn't wait to ask why Uncle Walter wanted him dead. He ran out of the house with Millie right behind him.

Uncle Walter cocked his rifle. "I'm gonna find that boy. I'm gonna find him and shoot him dead. He ain't never gonna bother a little girl again."

"Walter, sit down. I'll get you a glass of wine then we'll talk about this." Jonas wrestled the rifle out of Uncle Walter's hand.

As luck would have it, Mama waltzed in at the height of the chaos. "What in blazes is going on here?"

Jonas shouted at Mama. "No time to explain, Donna. Take Bertie home. I'll call tomorrow."

Mama grabbed my arm so hard I thought I'd never be able to use it again. She yanked me outside. "Get in the car. You best tell me what's going on in there, or I'll get your father's horse reins and beat you till you wish you'd never been born."

"I'm real scared, Mama. I've never seen Uncle Walter this fired up before. I didn't mean to cause trouble. Honest. I hope Jonas can get him calmed down."

"Not with alcohol, I hope. Your uncle's a drunk. Just because he hasn't had a bender in few years don't mean he'll never have one again. You'd better stay clear of my brother's house. Hear me?" She pulled the car onto the road then added, "Now tell me what happened, or you can go to Hades with the rest of them."

"Oh, Mama, it's my fault. I'm so sorry." The words tumbled like dead leaves in a gale, about Stoney, Millie, and how angry I got when Millie said Stoney got her pregnant. I wanted Mama to tell me I wasn't a bad person because I told on Millie. Only Mama didn't say a word. I hated myself so much I wanted her to get Papa's horse reins, beat me until she sent me to the devil like she'd promised.

Instead, she sent me to my room. "I'm too tired to discuss this tonight."

Afraid to cry, I fell into bed and stared out the window. Rain pelted against the pane. I wished I could be whisked away by a tornado like Dorothy to Oz. I didn't want to live in this world a minute longer. Since no storm came, I willed myself into an emotional black hole. I guessed God hated tattletales because they made more trouble than the trouble itself.

When I woke up, I forgot it was Christmas. Mama pounded on my door. When I didn't open it, she forced her way in then pulled me out of bed by my hair. "Get dressed, you harlot. You're coming with me. Walter won't answer my calls. I won't rest until I'm sure all's well over there."

I threw on a pair of slacks and a sweater. Mama didn't wait for me to get a coat and dragged me out to the car. I gripped the door handle and gasped for breath. I wanted to jump out of the car so I wouldn't have to face whatever was to come.

Mama pulled into Uncle Walter's driveway, parked, and got out, seemingly in one movement. "Follow me." While she ran, I hesitated before I gathered enough courage to open the passenger door. As she entered the house, her scream pierced the silence, the sound so loud the cows joined in her wails. She came back out then dragged me inside, her face red with fury. "See what you've done, you murderer."

A stench like a mountain of rotten apples filled the room.

Mama yanked my head toward the couch. "Look over there. This is your fault."

A man's body slumped on the couch, a red bandana puffed from his overalls and a rifle propped between his legs, his face blown away. Whiskey bottles littered the floor, blood stains streaked the walls, and a large pool of dark liquid coagulated on the carpet near his feet.

I looked away, but Mama yanked my face forward. "Don't you dare look away! You caused this trouble."

I closed my eyes, but when I opened them, reality slapped me in the face one more time. The dead man couldn't be Uncle Walter. When Leroy Atkins killed himself, Mama said, "Only cowards commit suicide." Uncle Walter was one of the bravest men I'd ever known.

"I'll call the troopers then wait for them outside. You stay here until they come."

I closed my eyes, but Mama punched me in the side. "You keep those eyes fixed on what you've done." She left me alone.to gaze upon horror.

I threw up in the sink. I wanted to be as dead as Uncle Walter. I went to the gun cabinet. Maybe I'd follow Uncle Walter's example, but there was no ammunition left. The distant sirens meant the police were on their way. I joined Mama outside as they pulled into the driveway.

One of the troopers asked to talk to Mama alone. The other talked to me. "You okay, Miss?"

I nodded.

He took out a notepad. "What's your name?"

"Bertha Brown. The woman with the other trooper is my mother, Donna Brown."

"I need to go inside for a few minutes. Do you want to go with me or wait out here?"

"I'll stay here."

I sat on the porch until the trooper returned. Seemed like Mama talked with the other trooper a long time. Why did they ask so many questions? Did she tell them how I killed the man inside?"

When the trooper came back, he talked with the other trooper then sat next to me. He had kind eyes. "Your mother said the dead man is her brother. Is that right?"

"Yes."

"She also said your uncle's friend and his daughter lived here. Any idea where either one might be?"

I thought maybe Jonas had gone to find Millie. He probably didn't know what Uncle Walter had done. I worried they might come back, find him dead, and blame me like Mama had. "No sir, I don't know where they went."

The trooper looked at me as if he knew I hadn't told the whole truth. I threw up on the step. He handed me his handkerchief and waited a couple of minutes before he asked more questions.

"I know this is hard for you. We're almost finished. There are decorations and left-over birthday cake in there. Was there a party here last night? Were you here?"

I tried to answer, but no words came out.

"Just nod or shake your head. Were you at the party last night?"

I nodded.

"Did this happen while you were there?"

I shook my head.

The trooper glanced at my mother. "Would you feel better if we talked where your mother can't hear you? We could go inside."

I'd rather be rained on by brimstone than set foot in Uncle Walter's house ever again. "I'd prefer to be out here, sir."

I pushed the words out and told him what happened, at least some of it. I left out the part about how I tattled on Millie and how jealous I was of her because she was pregnant with Stoney's baby, and I wasn't."

The trooper closed his notebook. "Thank you for the information."

By now, the other trooper left my mother and went into the house. She stood behind the trooper who questioned me. "If you don't need us any longer, I should take my daughter home now."

The trooper clicked his tongue. "I have no reason to hold you for now. An investigator will be in touch with you tomorrow."

When we got back into the car, Mama gripped the steering wheel with both hands.

"What will happen to Uncle Walter?" I asked.

"The morgue is on its way to pick the body up. There's nothing more we can do. When we get home, I want you to go straight to your room."

Instead of a tasty Christmas meal for Mama and me, I stayed in my bed all day and through the night. I didn't deserve to be alive, let alone eat."

I would have stayed in my room until I withered into oblivion if Mama would have let me. She might have, too, if investigators hadn't come to the house the next day. She barged into my room then hauled me out of bed to go talk to them. "They want to speak to you directly."

The younger one looked at me with sympathetic eyes but scowled at Mama as he talked. "We've been unable to locate Miss Cooper. We'll keep looking, of course, since she's a person of interest.

However, she's sixteen. There's very little we can do to convince her to come back home if she doesn't want to."

"I understand," Mama said.

The investigator continued. "Unfortunately, we found Jonas Gerard."

"Is he okay?" I asked though instinct told me he wasn't because he hadn't called like he'd promised.

The investigator shook his head. "I'm sorry, Mrs. Brown. We found Mr. Gerard's remains in Holcomb."

"Holcomb?" Mama asked. "Why on earth would Jonas be in Holcomb? It's a ghost town. What happened?"

"From what we can determine, his truck took a header off a bridge into the ravine below. If it helps to know, the coroner thinks he died on impact. He places the time of the accident early Christmas morning, perhaps one or two. Bertie, do you have any idea why Mr. Gerard was in Holcomb?"

I shook my head. "Maybe he went to look for my cousin. Only, she'd have no reason that I know of to go to Holcomb. Is it near Albany?"

"Yes, it is."

"We don't know anyone in Holcomb or Albany either," Mama said. If she'd been any more hostile, the investigator might have drawn his gun.

I admired his calm. "We contacted Mr. Gerard's brother who requested the remains be transported to Detroit for funeral arrangements there."

Mama clasped her hands together. "Thank you for keeping us informed. Jonas was my brother's friend. A God-fearing man, though he wasn't our family." Mama didn't get along with Uncle Walter, but everyone liked Jonas.

The investigator stood. "We'll let you know as soon as we find any information on the whereabouts of your niece."

"Don't bother. She probably ran off with that no good hired hand. I expect if you find him, you'll find her."

The older investigator shrugged. "So far we've come up empty on Stoney Rivers. The prints we found were a match to a man named Harry Stockwell. He's wanted on assault charges. Looks like your brother's hired hand fooled a lot of people. We've put out an APB."

Mama showed the detectives to the door. "I'm sure you'll do your best. If you do find my niece by any chance, tell her she can call us if she needs anything."

Mama's words most likely were said to impress the investigator, only I knew she didn't mean any of what she said. She'd never let Millie come live with us. Even if Mama had a change of heart, Millie would rather starve than accept help from either Mama or me.

Maybe Millie found Stoney or whatever his real name was, why no one could find her. Even if he was wanted by the police, I didn't think he'd be so cold as to not take care of his own baby. Most likely they went to New York City together. I'd heard if a person wanted to get lost, New York was the place to go.

Mama made arrangements for a private service with an undertaker from her church. Uncle Walter's coffin would be stored in a crypt until the graves opened in the spring.

"I won't be a hypocrite, Bertie. Your uncle made it clear he wanted no part of God, so why should I pretend he cares what happened? Walter killed himself, and God don't forgive suicide. Walter belongs to the devil now." Mama refused to go to the service but insisted I represent the two of us. "You killed him, Bertie. Now you stand vigil," she said after asking the funeral director to give me a ride home.

I stood next to his coffin as Mama demanded. "I'm sorry, Uncle Walter. I know you didn't kill yourself. The whiskey made you do this horrible thing. I wish you could know I never meant for any of these bad things to happen."

The funeral director took my hand. "Bertie, I'm sure in some way, he knows you didn't foresee any of these tragedies." He read The Twenty-Third Psalm then said a short prayer. Afterward, he took me home. I wanted to run away like Millie had done instead of going into the house. Maybe my punishment was to stay with Mama for the rest of my life.

She sat in the oversized living room chair. She stared at the carpet when I came in and refused to look at me. Tears finally came as I fell at Mama's feet.

"I'm so sorry, Mama. If I could take it all back, I would. Can't you forgive me?"

"No, Bertie. I will never forgive you. I'll do my Christian duty since you're still my responsibility. I'll give you a roof over your head and food to eat until you graduate. I don't want you in my house a day longer. I'll never forgive what you did to my brother."

Bertie
June
1963

Somehow I managed to finish school and graduated with a certificate in horticulture. Mama kept her word. I spent the next eighteen months as if I lived alone. She'd put out my supper plate as if I were a dog and made me eat by myself.

No one came to see Bertie Brown get her degree. When I returned home after graduation, Mama had locked herself up in her room. I shoved my diploma into my suitcase, along with my picture of Millie, and waited for my ride—my escape to my new, still undefined world.

Last night's hard rain now eased into a light mist. I blew relief at the sight of Mrs. Howard's black sedan. "Mama, I'm leaving now," I shouted. Not a word even now.

I thought how lucky I'd been to have a teacher like Mrs. Howard who taught my horticulture classes. Last month, she'd found me sitting in the corner of the girl's room. I thought maybe this would be the day I really did die. I couldn't stand one more day of Mama's silence. I'd rather she took out Papa's horse reins. She wasn't the only one who wished I'd never been born.

Mama always got mad if I cried, and I learned before I could walk how to cry so no one could hear me. Mrs. Howard led me to a private corner, held me and let me sob until I couldn't cry anymore.

After my breakdown in the girls' bathroom, I spoke with Mrs. Howard every day. She offered to give me a job at the local flower shop. I told her I wanted to get as far away from Cold Creek as I could. The week before graduation, she told me she'd found a job for me in Granite Falls at a tourist lodge. She knew the owners personally and thought they were nice people. I jumped at the chance to live in a place where no one knew me—a chance to start fresh.

When I got into the car, Mrs. Howard handed me an envelope. "Your mother sent this to me."

"Why you?"

"Now don't be upset, Bertie. The day I found you in the girls' bathroom, I spoke with your mother. I suggested the two of you see a counselor. Unfortunately, she refused. She did ask if I'd let her know where you would go after you graduated. So you see, your mother does care what happens to you. This is her way of saying she loves you."

When I opened the envelope, a fifty-dollar bill fell out. The note inside simply said, *Be sure Bertie gets this.*

"Guilt money. She used to send me cash when I lived at Uncle Walter's. I'm done with Mama, and she's done with me."

I stashed the money in my purse. I might need it. Since I had a job, this was the last she'd send money. I was completely on my own from this day forward.

For the next two hours, Mrs. Howard filled me in on my employers. I welcomed her chit chat. "You'll love Antonio Bartonelli and his wife. I worked at *La Roma* during my summer vacations. They treated me like a daughter."

"Is Antonio really Italian?"

Mrs. Howard laughed. "No one knows for sure. He might have Italian ancestry. He legally changed his name from Anthony Barton to Antonio Bartonelli when he inherited the lodge from his wealthy father-in-law. Before Antonio took over, the place was known as *The Hideaway,* frequented by famous celebrities like Frank Sinatra and John Wayne."

I warmed to think I'd have a job at a place where actors once visited.

"Everyone in Granite Falls adores Antonio."

"What about his wife?"

"Her given name was Lucille. Now she is known as Lucia."

"Why change their names?"

"All part of the show, what draws people to *La Roma*."

"Show?"

"Antonio wanders through the restaurant and plays the violin. Sometimes he performs a few opera arias. Rumor is he did a short stint at the Met before he married Lucille."

As Mrs. Howard talked, I pictured what life might be like in Granite Falls. "I spent an afternoon at the library. I didn't know Granite Falls had been a mining town."

"At one time it was. The depression hit upstate New York pretty hard. Half the population moved out. Probably why the town gets behind *La Roma*. It's still a tourist attraction, though not the celebrity draw it once was. Antonio and Lucia aren't exactly spring chickens."

Mrs. Howard parked the car. "Ready to start your new life?"

I nodded. Any place had to be better than Cold Creek.

I gawked at the finery like a country boy stares at skyscrapers in the city. Mrs. Howard led me through a maze of halls then knocked on the door of a small apartment. A woman, perhaps in her late sixties, not quite as wide as the space between the door jams, greeted us. She drew Mrs. Howard into a long embrace. "My dear Emma. So good to see you."

The woman's smile warmed me like hot apple cider. "This must be Bertie." She pulled me in for a quick hug, and I thought I'd drown within her fleshy arms.

Mrs. Howard gave me a farewell hug. "My job here is done. You're in good hands. Please let me know how you're doing."

"I promise to write."

She left, and with her went my last connection to past worlds. I turned to my newly adopted mother. "Thank you for your kindness, Mrs. Bartonelli."

"We're happy to have a young girl in our home once more." She took my suitcase. "Come, follow me. I'll show you to your room."

As she turned, a short, thin, nearly bald man came into the apartment. He took off his chef's hat and with a twist, tossed it on a nearby chair. "Ah, so this is our new charge." He kissed me on the cheek. I blushed at his familiarity, yet welcomed affection. From his phony accent, I assumed the man must be Antonio.

"What do you want me to call you?"

"Why Mama Lucia and Papa Antonio, of course," Lucia answered. "No need for formality here. Consider us your parents. Let's get you settled in. Papa Antonio needs to work on the books."

He tilted his head then tweaked Lucia's cheek. "Yes … no … whatever this beautiful woman wants me to say."

Mama Lucia led the way to what would be my bedroom. I gasped at the luxury, like a scene from *Gone with the Wind*. A lacy canopy bed took up most of the room while French doors opened onto a veranda. Marble-topped nightstands stood at either side of the bed, and a cedar wardrobe filled the room with a pleasant aroma, like the cedar hedges from home. My eyes misted at my good fortune. "Oh, Mama Lucia, the room is lovely, far more than what I deserve."

"Oh, shush. A beautiful girl like you deserves a beautiful room. Papa Antonio and I never had any children so we are glad to be foster parents from time to time."

"Will I start tomorrow?"

"There's no hurry. If you feel you're ready, tomorrow it is. Now I'll leave you to unpack. Then come join us for ice cream before you go to bed."

When Mama Lucia left, I sunk onto the bed. What had I done to deserve this kindness? How soon before the nightmare of my life resumed? I couldn't be sure about my future. Yet, for the first time since I left Uncle Walter's farm, I felt wanted. I didn't know how to pray, so I lifted my hands in gratitude to heaven. "Thank you for this haven. But if it's not too much to ask, would you help me find Millie?"

Ryan
Christmas Eve
1999

Mom wiped her eyes. So far, none of what she said explained my father's absence. Yet, even a thick-headed factory worker like me could see why she lost any ability to cope. I supposed too many losses in life sucks the fight out of a person. Could this be behind Penny's sadness—a past trauma she refused to share with anyone?

If only she'd talk to me.

Mom lined the counter with powdered sugar and sundry items—this time to make frosting for Millie's cake. Of all the images of my mother I recall after we moved back to Granite Falls, most would include her at the kitchen counter. As much as I wanted to hear more, I knew she needed a break from painful memories.

I deluded myself with pride. Whatever sins I might have committed in my nearly twenty-nine years, I was a better man than Stoney Rivers.

Mom stared at the ceiling like R.J. does when he's about to compose a deep thought. "I know worry doesn't do a bit of good. But I never could stop my worry over what happened to Millie and her baby. When you were born, I wished she could know I had a baby too."

"I'm glad she's found you. Don't spend so much time in the past, though. Life is hard enough. No need to drudge up old wounds."

Penny's glance froze my heart while my mother only scowled. "Hear what you just said, Ryan? Maybe you should listen to your own advice."

As a kid, I acted without forethought, mostly out of anger. Perhaps some force in the universe looked out for angry kids. I suppose I'd been fortunate enough to have angels in my life, folks who came in human forms like Gina Forbes, Belle Thompson, and Officer Doty. Would there be angels for R.J. if I could no longer be there for him?

As I thought of Belle Thompson's personal God, I whispered a prayer, not sure if it would be heard. I asked this unknown God to watch out for my son in my absence. Maybe in weakness, or in desperation, Mom had prayed for me. Was it possible somewhere on this earth, in some distant part of the globe, my father, if he still lived, prayed for us?

Belle Thompson said I'd have doubts about God for as long as I chose anger over the healing God could give. "Life doesn't come wrapped up in pretty bows, Ryan," she said to me the day Officer Doty took me to her place to sweep floors as part of my informal probation. "The sooner you can learn to accept accountability for your own actions, the better off you'll be. Every person who ever took a breath in this world has had disappointment. Time you let yourself mend."

I ignored her advice.

I wondered if Mom refused to listen to her angels as I had turned a deaf ear to mine.

"Antonio and Lucia sounded like really special folks. How long did you stay there? Are they still alive?"

"I don't know about Mama Lucia, I doubt it. Papa Antonio died soon after I got married. Lucia moved to Florida. She wrote for a few years. The letters stopped when she went to a nursing home. Ryan, did I ever tell you how I met your father?"

Bertie
1968

The office at *La Roma* became my second home. I didn't mind the bookwork as it kept my mind occupied. I bent over a pile of paperwork to transcribe numbers from receipts payable into ledgers. Mama Lucia pushed the books aside. "I never see you go out, not even to a movie. You're too young to let your life slip away with only work."

I pulled the books back to finish the entries. "I'm happy, Mama Lucia. Both you and Papa Antonio have been very good to me. I read, and Papa Antonio teaches me how to cook. What more do I need?"

"How about a boyfriend?"

I shuddered as I remembered Stoney.

"I don't need a boyfriend. At least not right now. I almost have enough money to start my own restaurant in Albany. I don't need some jerky boyfriend to ruin my dreams."

"Why open up your own restaurant when you can stay here with us?"

A part of me wanted to stay. However, I needed to fly on my own sooner or later. *La Roma* barely broke even the previous year. If these receipts were any indicator, business hadn't picked up in recent months.

Since I'd never become an actress, a new dream took the place of the old. With the highway expansion, why not open a chain of stores in key spots near the exits to include a café—a convenient place for travelers?

Antonio and Lucia were independently wealthy, and *La Roma* was more of a hobby than a business. From what I read, many large Adirondack resorts teetered on bankruptcy. Mountain visitors' quests now veered toward outdoor adventures like boating, hiking, and golf instead of the lodge experience. When I suggested Antonio adapt the venue to appeal to sportsmen, he squelched the idea. "Hunters and fisherman would not be happy with violins and opera. *La Roma* is a place of romance, not baseball. My customers want to hear Verde, not Pete Rose's statistics."

For the present, *La Roma* provided me with contentment in spite of Papa Antonio's persistent efforts to find me a mate. He set up blind dates with a few of his friends, older men he thought would provide well for me. I suspected he wanted me to marry one of his die-hard customers so I'd stay in Granite Falls to produce a surrogate grandchild.

Mama Lucia would not let the matter of my non-existent social life drop. "Don't be angry, Bertie. There is a very nice young man we want you to meet, a handsome boy closer to your age."

Before I could refuse, Papa Antonio lumbered into the room, accompanied by a tall man with dark hair. His confident walk reminded me of Stoney. I'd asked Mrs. Howard not to tell my benefactors about my uncle or my relationship with his hired hand. How would they know why I froze when I first saw Ian McDougal?

Papa Antonio introduced us. "Ian is our new handyman."

I tried in vain to avoid his deep-set brown eyes as he tugged his hat. "Howdy-do."

Antonio beamed with pride, like Uncle Walter when he hired Stoney. "Lots of things need to be fixed around here. I'm too old to do it all myself."

I turned to Antonio. "Where will Mr. McDougal live?"

"I promised him a room at the lodge. Ian's new in town."

Didn't Papa Antonio read the sign on my heart, *Beware of Strangers*?

I liked Ian's drawl, part western, part southern. I also liked the way he positioned his hat when he talked like some people gesture with their hands.

"Do you have references, Mr. McDougal?"

Ian frowned at my frostiness. "In fact, I do, ma'am."

Antonio pulled out a résumé. "Right here, Bertie. He used to be a truck driver."

"So why did you leave? A trucker makes a lot more money than a handyman."

Ian laughed. "Antonio asked me the same question. I didn't expect I'd have to endure a second interview once he offered me the job. I'll tell you exactly what I told Antonio. I studied to be a mechanical engineer. I didn't like school, so I went to work for Transcontinental Trucking. I got tired of the open road. I always liked the Adirondacks, and I've made deliveries in Granite Falls. These mountains remind me of the Rockies. I decided I wanted to put down roots. Granite Falls seemed as good a place as any. Now you've got my history. What's yours?"

My cheeks heated, and I turned away to hide my embarrassment, or maybe my attraction. Ian McDougal got to me in a way no other man had since Stoney. I made up my mind to stay clear of any man with a confident swagger.

As the weeks sped by, Ian became a fixture at *La Roma*. Whenever he came into the office, I purposefully kept my face buried in the ledgers, especially when he tried to engage me in small talk. I did my best to avoid his glances yet became infatuated with how his tool belt fell onto perfectly formed hips.

One day, Papa Antonio came into the office while Ian poured himself a cup of coffee. As usual, I struggled to ignore him while he chatted with Papa Antonio. "Ian, Lucia told me you play the guitar?"

"I haven't in a few years. I used to be in a band. Why do you ask?"

"Do you sing opera?"

Ian laughed. "Sorry. I was born in Tennessee before my folks moved to Oklahoma. I'm afraid I'm a country boy."

"Well, here's the thing. My voice isn't what it used to be. I think I need a new act on stage. Want the gig? Friday and Saturday nights."

"I could use the extra money. I'd like to buy a house in town. If you don't mind a few yodels instead of arias, we have a deal."

When Antonio left, Ian sat on my desk, the closest he'd come to me since Antonio hired him. "You don't seem pleased at Antonio's offer."

"It's not my concern."

"Will you stay to listen? I could use a good critic like you."

If he hadn't smiled when he'd spoke, I'd have slapped him. "What do you mean?"

"I mean, Bertie Brown, I'd like to see your pretty face when I sing love songs."

I leaned back in my chair. "Is this a pass, Ian McDougal?"

"Why do you think I've taken your cold shoulder for the last month, why I come into the office so much? I don't even like coffee."

My hands trembled, and my feet readied to walk out, but my heart trumped my resistance. He kissed me. I didn't resist. "Tonight. Dinner. Not here, though. I'll pick you up at seven."

Before I could answer, he swaggered out.

I'd always suspected Papa Antonio listened outside the office whenever Ian and I talked. Papa Antonio burst in and clapped his hands. "Bertie, go on, get out of here. It's five o'clock. Go get ready for your date. You will want to change, no?"

"Into what?"

"Don't you have a pretty dress to wear?"

"I don't believe in fairy tales, and you're not my Godmother. It's only dinner."

🍁

"Another date with Ian?" Antonio asked as I hurried from the office. "You have a certain telltale glow, Bertie."

"Only because my makeup wore off. I'll be sure to powder my nose before I go out tonight."

"Maybe I should give him the weekends off for a while?"

"No need."

"Where to ?"

"To see *2001: A Space Odyssey*. Ian's a big science-fiction fan. He's excited it's finally made its way to Granite Falls."

Antonio grinned.

"What? I enjoy his company. It's nice to have a friend."

"Papa Antonio knows. Ian wants to be more than your friend."

"I'm not ready for more. Maybe I'll never be."

Mama Lucia came in with a stack of receipts. "These can wait until tomorrow, Bertie." She smiled. "You have more important things to do tonight. Besides, I have a date, too." She kissed Papa Antonio, and he twirled her around. They waltzed to his rendition of *O Sole Mio*.

"You two are lucky to still be in love after all these years together."

"You don't think you'll find love?"

"Everyone I've loved either died or ran away. Even my dog, Charlie. He left the day after my father died. I don't want to fall in love. It hurts too much."

Mama Lucia drew me into one of her strong embraces "Don't talk so, Bertie. If you keep your heart in a box, you'll wither away. It is true, sometimes love makes a heart break. But it will break from something. Such is the way of life. Better to love and lose than to never have known the sweet caress of a man's arms."

I remembered Stoney. Did I dare allow myself to love another man? "What do you think, Papa Antonio?"

"I think love is always worth the risk. Where would I be today if I hadn't followed my heart?" He kissed his wife's hand. "Did you know today is our fiftieth anniversary?"

Was it possible to love someone so passionately for so many decades?

Did I love Ian McDougal, the man whose smile rivaled Robert Redford, who sang like Elvis, and played the guitar like Chet Akins?

Only time would tell. He'd kissed me the night before—a nice kiss. I wanted more. Not like it had been with Stoney. His kisses demanded release. Ian held me tenderly, with no expectation I return his passion until ready.

How long would he wait? He'd said he wanted to put down roots. What about my dream? Did I want to forsake another life ambition and remain in Granite Falls?

🍁

After the movie, we stopped at the Main Street Diner for a hamburger. Ian picked a booth toward the back of the restaurant. I played with the sugar container.

He lifted my chin as he met my gaze. "You're deep in thought. Care to let me know what's new in Bertie World?"

"It's a ghost town, I'm afraid."

He laughed. "Did you enjoy the movie?"

"Mostly, though I did find it a little hard to follow."

"What did you thank of Hal?"

"Scary."

"I foresee a time in the not too far future when computers will take over the world. With so much technological advancement, I wouldn't be surprised if, in our lifetime, house phones become obsolete."

I smiled. "You think we'll all run around with communicators like on Star Trek?"

"Absolutely."

"I'd miss getting tangled up in the phone cord."

Ian's grin pulled me every which way but sane. "Soon everyone will have a computer in their house, small ones, not like those crazy standup ones they're working on now. I expect cars will have computers too."

"I don't think I want to live in a world as you describe. We might lose the ability to have a normal conversation with people.

Neighbors won't sit with each other on front porches and share a cup of coffee. We night lose the ability to talk at all."

Ian brought my hand to his lips. "So long as they don't replace kissing."

"Do you think we'll ever send a man to the moon?"

"We have to keep up with the Russians, don't we?" He tilted his cap to one side, like a cocky teenager. "Americans dominate in every other arena. Might as well be champions in space, too."

I thought about my champions, like Papa Antonio. "Are you happy here at *La Roma*?"

"As long as you're there, I am."

"Have you ever thought of doing something else?"

"Absolutely."

"What?"

"I want to start a family—with you. I love you, Bertie."

What could I say? I leaned back against the booth. "It's too soon to speak of love."

He set his cap next to him then gently gripped my chin. "Here's what I think, Bertie Brown. I think you love me too, though you're afraid to admit you do. For me, this is the real deal—not an infatuation. When a man finds the right woman, he doesn't have to think about it very long. When it's right, it's right. I know where you and I are concerned, it's right. I will wait as long as it takes for you to be as sure as I am."

I shoved his hand away. "Ian, I can't talk about this."

"You can't or you won't? I don't want this to be a fling. Bertie. I want to marry you."

"Ian—stop right there."

"I get it. Someone hurt you. You're afraid to trust me. Maybe someday you'll tell me about it. Until then, know this, Bertie Brown. You won't find another man who loves you as much as I do."

Ryan
Christmas Eve
1999

Were my parents once happy?

Before Pop left, I thought so. I woke to love every day, and Mom had fresh biscuits on the table. After breakfast, my father put on his yellow hard hat, mussed my hair, and told me to take good care of my mother until he returned. He bent my mother back to kiss her. Mom hurried to the kitchen window to blow him a kiss as he got into his truck.

"Did you take good care of your mother, Sport?" he asked as soon as he got home.

I liked being the man of the house while he was gone.

What stole love from Maple Street?

Mom took out candles from the cupboard and placed them on Millie's cake. Maybe her thoughts wandered to happier Christmases as mine had done. "Weatherman says it'll be warm tomorrow."

I figured there were only a few more layers to peel before I reached the meat of truth.

Penny's glare ping-ponged from me to Mom.

"What's wrong?" I asked.

"I need to say goodnight to R.J."

As she left, I wanted to follow her to see if she would talk. I rose.

She turned. "No, Ryan. I know you want to go upstairs with me, to take me to your room, to be like we used to be. I don't see how we can ever be like we once were."

We both fought a war. I was supposed to be her protector, to keep her safe, love her until death parted us. Instead, somehow, I caused her to want to leave me.

Mom poured another cup of coffee then brought it over. "Let her go, Ryan. Some battles have to be fought alone."

When Penny's war ended, would I lose both her and R.J. for good?

Mom wiped her hands on her apron. "Think I'll go air out the spare room, in case Millie decides to sleep here. Fresh air is nature's cleanser."

Left to myself, I fought the demons in my mind, afraid to know why my wife despised me as well as afraid to know why my father ruined my happy childhood. Mom said he'd been a good man, a hero to me. How could he walk away?

When I shaved this morning, I realized how much I resembled him. Like father like son? Perhaps in some ways. I remembered a fishing trip we'd taken the summer before he disappeared. I'd hooked a big trout. I fought him for five minutes. Instead of taking the line, Pop let me struggle. Then he said, "You'll know when to reel him in. Listen to your gut." Instinct told me to yank and reel, and confidence helped me find the strength to bring my catch home. Pop mussed my hair. "See what I mean? Trust your gut … when it feels right, then jerk the line."

I understood what he meant when he told Mom how a man is certain he's found the woman he'll love forever. I fell head over heels with Penny the first minute I saw her. My buddy, Goose Reinhardt, and few other soldiers decided to come to Atlanta for a few days to celebrate my birthday. We hit the Oasis on the first night. I'm sure I wasn't the only soldier to be attracted to a girl like Penny. When she came to our table, she flirted with me a little. "Be sure to stick around, Mountain Boy," she'd said. Maybe she only asked to be polite. I knew I wanted to be with her the rest of my life.

I jerked the line.

"Best birthday present I could get would be if you joined us for coffee after your last set."

"You're on, Mountain Boy."

We went to the diner next door. Goose whispered in my ear. "You got this, buddy. See you back at the base tomorrow night."

I must have downed five cups of coffee while Penny and I talked. As the sun rose, she suggested we go back to her apartment. When we left, I think we both knew we'd never be apart. She fell asleep in my arms. Though we hadn't made love, I thought we fit together like puzzle pieces. I called the base to request an extended leave. Five days after we met, the question popped out. "Why don't we drive to Vegas to get married?"

"Why Vegas? It's nearly all the way across the country. I've got a better idea. Let's go to Alabama. A friend of mine went there to get married. No wait time or blood test required. The age requirement is only sixteen. All we have to do is find a judge. We can be married tomorrow. Don't need any witnesses, and we don't have to be Alabama residents."

"Sounds great. Let's go."

We hopped into my truck to our fairy tale ending. Now, I worried my marriage was no longer the happily forever after I'd thought it would be.

Mom and Penny came back in together.

"How's R.J.?" I asked. "Asleep yet?"

Penny went to the sink to wash R.J.'s dessert plates.

"He's too excited to sleep."

Mom gazed out the window. "Sure hope Millie finds the place without any problem." Another diversion? I'd have to prod Mom's thoughts if I were to keep her on task. "Mom, you and Pop were happy, at first, weren't you?"

"I'd like to think so. Don't be so hard on your father. I'm the one who lied. After he had blurted out his intention, he posed the question nearly every time we went out. I knew eventually I'd say yes."

Bertie
Summer
1969

By summer *La Roma* closed, except for special events. Ian and I spent most of our nights with Mama Lucia and Papa Antonio. By this time, Ian found a job as a lineman for the telephone company. The hours were a little crazy, but the pay was good, and Ian edged closer to his goal to buy property in town.

We'd come to Mama Lucia's to watch the lunar landing. I held Muffin, Mama Lucia's three-colored, seven-toed cat, on my lap. She panted, about to give birth. I laid her in a box I'd prepared ahead since her time was near. Some mother cats hide. Not Muffin. She wanted me right there until her sixth baby popped out. My cheeks were wet as I watched the miracle of birth. Muffin could care less that history unfolded before us.

Ian called to me. "Bertie, come here. They're about to take their walk." As much as I'd come to love history, Muffin's babies intrigued me more. I watched as their tired mother found the impossible strength to give her babies their first bath. She purred as they suckled with closed eyes.

"Hurry up, Bertie," Ian called again. "They'll be out of the capsule any minute. Seems like science-fiction, but it's real life, baby." Ian pulled me away from Muffin and onto the couch as Neil Armstrong uttered his memorable words, "That's one small step for man, one giant leap for mankind."

Ian laughed. "Come sit with us. This is bigger than birthing kittens."

"I think Muffin disagrees."

He looked into my eyes. "What's inside that pretty head of yours, baby?"

A beautiful event happened while the world's eyes turned elsewhere. Maybe since an early age, Armstrong knew he'd be the first man to walk on the moon. Good for him. He lived to see his dream come true. What if a dream changed? As a teenager, all I wanted to be was an actress. After a few years at *La Roma*, I developed a more grown up dream—to become a successful business woman. As I watched Muffin birth her babies, a new dream awakened. Like Ian, I wanted a family. I determined I would no longer let yesterday's nightmare rob me of today's blessings.

I put my head on my love's shoulder. "Ian McDougal, your Eagle has landed."

He kissed me, and we missed the golf match on the moon as we gazed into each other's eyes. He turned to Papa Antonio. "How soon can we book a party at *La Roma*?"

Papa Antonio twirled to face us. "Whenever you want. What's the occasion?"

We announced our engagement in sync. "We're getting married."

Mama Lucia turned off history and clapped for joy. "I'll call Reverend Duvall right now. Bertie, you leave everything to me and Papa Antonio."

🍁

I glanced at my long white gown while Mama Lucia splashed my face with glitter. Soon I'd be a married woman. Papa Antonio wasted no expense on our reception, as proud to give me away as I'd hoped my real Papa would have been if he'd lived. There wouldn't be many guests—a few of Ian's coworkers as well as friends of the Bartonellis. Except for Millie, I had no one else to invite, no way to find out where she might be.

Thoughts of Millie reminded me of what Stoney had taken from me. I blushed with remembered shame. A white dress was supposed to symbolize purity—my dress, a brazen lie.

I never told Ian about Stoney or my life in Cold Creek. He only knew I didn't get along well with my mother and how a teacher had found my job at *La Roma*. I couldn't tell anyone about Stoney and how my foolishness caused Uncle Walter and Jonas' deaths. Better to leave all those memories in the dark dungeons of my soul.

I froze with the thought. What would I do when Ian took me to his bed? He believed me to be innocent. If he knew I'd been with a man before him, he would want to know who, and he might feel he had to be a better lover than any other man I'd been with. For the best if Ian never knew there'd been a man in my life named Stoney Rivers. When the time came, I'd pretend innocence and let Ian teach me.

Papa Antonio knocked at my dressing room door. "Can the surrogate father of the bride come in?"

I thought how happy I'd been since I came to *La Roma*. Who better than Papa Antonio to give me away? "Of course."

He handed me a document. "This is our gift to our beautiful daughter."

Mama Lucia smiled. Her eyes twinkled like a mischievous fairy as she took my bouquet. "Read it."

I trembled at their generosity. "You bought a house for us?"

"On Maple Street. I heard the two of you looked at the house last week, but Ian didn't have enough saved for the down payment."

"Does he know?"

"He's excited and can't wait to fill it with children. Who knows, maybe Papa Antonio will have a grandchild to bounce on his knee before the Lord calls him home?"

Ryan
Christmas Eve
1999

Bitterness turned my throat dry. "I don't understand. If you and Pop were so happy, what did you do to make him leave?"

I sensed the venom in my voice. My mother recoiled as if I'd punched her in the gut.

As a boy, I thought Pop left because I'd disappointed him. Mom owned blame for his desertion.

She wiped the tears from her eyes and glared at Penny but spoke to me. "Ryan, a marriage based on a lie is doomed to fail. Your father left me … not you."

Bertie
Christmas Eve
1978

I failed to notice Ian as he came into the bedroom. I clutched Millie's photograph to my chest, overwhelmed with grief. Today was her birthday. How I missed her. I tried to find joy in the usual fuss of the Holiday, but all I wanted to do was to crawl into bed and never wake up. With every present I wrapped, the images of Millie's sixteenth birthday and Uncle Walter's suicide revisited. Whenever I threw away a rotten apple, the stench of death lingered for days.

I could no longer pretend I was happy. Ian must have sensed my mood, especially when I stumbled from the table. When he came in, he found me stretched out on the bed, Millie's picture tight against my heart.

He pried the picture from my grip. "Time to let go, baby, before you lose circulation." You've held the frame so tight against you, you've left an imprint on your dress." He forced me to a stand. "It's Christmas Eve. This isn't like you, Bertie. Come sing Christmas carols with us. I'll put Ryan to bed, and then we'll talk. Okay?"

I shivered, not because of the cold. An icy spirit possessed me. "I'm lost in memories." "About the girl in the picture?"
I nodded.

He led me to the living room where you played with your trucks. We must have sung *Rudolph the Red-Nosed Reindeer* half a dozen times, your favorite. Ian ended with *Silent Night*.

Only peace of any kind eluded me.

"Stay here, Bertie, while I put Ryan to bed. It's time you told me what happened to Millie. You've kept me in the dark far too long. Truth has to come out sooner or later, or it eats you alive."

While Ian tucked you into bed, I rocked back and forth as if the chair were a time machine to take me back to a fateful night and let me design a different future than the one I'd been forced to live. I became this other person who heard my cries, "I'm so sorry, Millie. I'm so sorry."

"What are you sorry about, Bertie?" Ian said when he returned.

If I told Ian why Millie ran away, I'd have to tell him about Stoney, how Uncle Walter killed himself, how Jonas died when he went after Millie. Two people died, and Millie ran away, all because of me. If I'd never made love to Stoney, none of those things would have happened.

Ian pulled me to a stand. "Come into the kitchen. I'll make you a cup of tea then you can tell me about Millie. This picture's possessed you. It has to end. Tonight."

I was trapped, like a squealing mouse in a death rattle. I either had to tell Ian the truth or go insane. No matter what I chose to do, I knew my world was about to end. I'd rather die first. Only death, no matter how I wished for it, wouldn't come.

My life with Ian had been wonderful to this point, as wonderful as could be hoped for given the lie between us. Every day was like a honeymoon. Ian called me when he left work then I'd wait for him by the kitchen window. As soon as he came through the door, he showered me with kisses, even if you were near. After you had learned to walk, Ian included you in the daily rituals.

Ian placed a cup of hot tea in front of me. I defied the moment. "I need to wash the dinner dishes."

"Never mind. Talk to me. Time we both faced whatever this is … if it takes all night."

Somehow I summoned long delayed truth. I glanced at Millie's picture. "She was the best friend I ever had." I trembled so hard I started to fall from the chair. Ian put his arms around me, his love my support. "Do you know how much I love you and Ryan?"

He nodded.

"I'm afraid, Ian."

"Of what?"

"I've lost so much. Papa died when I was twelve. Then Mama got to be so mean. After she died, I couldn't get Millie out of my head. I miss her so. I don't know what happened to her after she ran away."

"Didn't you have two brothers?"

"John died in Vietnam a year before I graduated. Since my mother refused to talk to me, I found out about him in the school newspaper. I don't know where Verne is. Mama got a letter with a return address from Nashville. I saw it unopened on the kitchen table. Later, I saw it ripped up in the trash, too many pieces to put back together. I never knew what Verne had done to make Mama so mad at him. I didn't have an address to write to him, either."

"Maybe you're sad because you miss your brothers?"

"I have you and Ryan. It's enough, isn't it?"

"I think you need answers. If you want, I'll ask my boss for a temporary transfer to Nashville. Maybe we can find Verne at least."

"Could we take a trip this summer, after school lets out?"

"Would you like to?"

I nodded.

In spite of Ian's hopeful promise, guilt still overwhelmed me. I'd lied to the most wonderful man on earth. He had to know about Stoney. Falsehoods ate me inside out. "Do you think there'd be any way I could find Millie?"

"Why are you so obsessed with a cousin you haven't seen in years? The girl ran away for a reason. She probably doesn't want to be found. You have to respect her wishes, Bertie."

"You're right, and I should let her be, but I can't. I need to know what happened to her."

"Why?"

For all of Ian's tenderness, he remained prideful. He insisted a man should be head of his household as a teacher and leader. He believed this wisdom defined us in bed and as a couple.

How could I confess my lack of innocence and not destroy his love for me? How would he react to know his wife caused two people to die and ruined the life of another?

"Bertie, tell me."

I clutched Millie's picture to my chest once more. "Okay. I'll tell you. Millie was the best friend I ever had before Stoney Rivers came to work for my uncle, my mother's brother—"

The words flowed hot off my tongue as I found courage I never knew before. As I spoke, his eyes widened, and he panted like a woman in labor as his face turned three shades deeper than crimson. I expected his anger, but not to the heights it raged.

"Ian. You're scaring me. I'm sorry I lied to you."

He rose and cursed as he paced. In his rampage, he kicked each piece of furniture and punched the walls. He called me names I thought I'd never hear him say, "Whore … Jezebel." His words cut deeper than Papa's horse reins. "You know what the worst part is, Bertie? I don't care you weren't a virgin when we married. I can't forgive how you made a fool of me with your lies. I don't think I can ever trust you again."

My heart shattered as he slammed the door on our lives together.

Ryan
Christmas Eve
1999

A good son would have reassured his mother, let her know she was loved; and tell her whatever happened between husband and wife, she could never destroy her son's love. I meant to say those words.

However, before Mom could catch her breath, Penny bolted to her room, her sobs ominous. "Oh, God. Oh, God."

I looked at my mother. "What's wrong with her?" I pulled out the picture from my pocket. "Is it about this?"

"I think so. You need to go to her. Right now. She needs you."

I went to her temporary room, afraid to open the door to truth, weaponless against the forces threatening to tear us apart.

Her silhouette of despair filled the wall behind her bed.

"Penny?"

She paced, her pleas a whip to my heart. "Oh, God. Oh, God." She scratched her arms. "I can't. I can't."

I led her back to her bed then turned on her bedside lamp. "What's wrong?"

She looked away.

I gently moved her head in my direction then showed her the picture.

She gurgled. "Where did you find it?"

"In the shed, stuck underneath the door. I found it when I went out to play catch with R.J."

She grabbed the picture from my hand and threw it to the floor.

"Ryan. Go away. I can't look at you."

"What did I do? Whatever it was, I'm sorry. Can't we fix this? I love you."

"No. It's not you, Ryan. I'm the sinner in this story."

"Nonsense. You're the saintliest person I know. You and Belle Thompson."

"I love you, Ryan. I have since the day we met. I love you more now than ever."

"Yet, you can't look at me. If you love me, don't you think I deserve an explanation?"

She turned to face me, her eyes big with fear. "Yes, you do. Even if I lose you. You see, I understand why your father left your mother. You're more like your father than what you want to admit. Every bit as prideful."

"Penny, sit down. We'll find a way to work through this, whatever this is."

She sat then took three deep breaths. "Something happened to me a week before we met—something so bad I had put it from my mind. At least, I thought so until the picture came in the mail."

"Who sent it?"

"Chris Tooley. He thought I'd like the memento. He meant to be kind. Problem is, the picture jarred memories long buried."

"Talk to me."

"Your mother's right, you know. Truth can't stay hidden forever."

Penny made no sense. Didn't she realize how much she meant to me? When we married, I believed no power on earth could separate us. How could a simple picture spell disaster? Maybe she should keep her secret. Rebury it, get on with our lives. As I gazed into her eyes, I knew, for her sake, this barrier had to come down.

She trembled.

"Are you worried you weren't a virgin when we got married? Good grief. It's a new day. I wouldn't leave you because you'd been with another man or even if you'd kept your previous boyfriends a secret from me. You have to believe me."

Her eyes welled with newfound tears. "If only it were so simple." Her head drooped. "Your father left your mother because she lied to him."

"Did you lie to me about something?"

"Sort of."

"What?"

She breathed a long, hard sigh. "Ryan, the something that happened to me before we met—I was raped."

I don't know what came over me. My mind had been tossed around the whole day. I froze. I wanted to be there for Penny, to listen as I had patiently listened to my mother. What a good husband should do.

I wasn't that man. I walked out, suddenly sympathetic of my father's rage … how badly betrayal stung … especially by the woman he loved … deceit the hardest truth to bear. However horrible Penny's rape might have been for her, one thought consumed me. R.J., my namesake, the light of my life, was not mine.

I skidded out of the driveway onto the road headlong to nowhere. I meandered through back roads in search of a cliff to drive off, tired of the lies, tired of the women whose stupid choices had brought me to this moment of desperation.

Maybe instinct takes over when reason leaves or maybe my will to live was stronger than my death wish. I found myself in front of Belle's Café, surprised it was still open this late on Christmas Eve. Then again, I wouldn't be surprised if Belle purposefully kept the place available for lonely souls in need of a kind word. Belle might be the only person in Granite Falls I could trust to straighten out the tangled mess in my head.

A burly hunter sat in my usual spot. Belle pointed to the tables in the back. I took a seat and mused over my strange relationship with a fifty-year-old former nun. When Belle opened up her place, town people gossiped she'd left the order because of a love affair gone wrong.

Maybe the rumors were true, no one knew for sure. I think Belle saw the café as a ministry, a chance to serve apart from a nun's habit. She liked to listen while downtrodden folks poured out their troubles. Though the café resembled a sport's bar, complete with pool tables, darts, and five wide-screen televisions, Belle's atmosphere seemed more like a church. She only served non-alcoholic specialty drinks and kept a Bible on a table near the fireplace. I never picked it up, though Belle encouraged me to more than once.

Belle claimed she counseled more people in a day than the town's mental health clinic. Rumors were she graduated from Columbia with a degree in psychology. Her only rule—no one could ask her personal questions, though everyone in Granite Falls knew she lived the life she preached. "I don't consider myself a religious person," she'd say. "I'm merely a Christian."

Made no sense. How were Christians not religious?

Belle cared about people. She hired the homeless and gave delinquent waifs like me a second chance. I stayed on at Belle's even after my probation ended. She cried the day I enlisted.

Belle's Café had been my true home since I turned fourteen. Only natural I ended up at her place now. She served the hunter the house specialty, the lumberjack breakfast plate, then brought two cups of coffee to my table. "I haven't seen you look so beaten since John Doty brought you to work for me."

I smirked.

"Yep. Same look. I need to close up pretty soon, send my cook home to his family for Christmas Eve. You want to talk. Talk. If you came in here to pout, there's the door."

I spewed the day's events like a kid reviews his favorite movie, an embellished, one-sided interpretation. "Thing is, Belle, if what Penny said is true, R.J.'s probably not my kid. How could she lie to me? She let me brag to everyone we met how I had the smartest son in Granite Falls when she knew full well I couldn't take credit for his intelligence."

Belle slapped my head. "Ryan McDougal, you have to be the biggest jerk this side of Albany."

I'd come for sympathy, not condemnation.

"You need to understand, Ryan, rape is the worst assault on a woman there is."

I supposed I did understand on some level. I wished, for Penny's sake, I could get past my selfish rage. "I'm sorry some creep took advantage of her. She still had no right to deceive me about R.J." Anger rose again as I condemned my wife when in truth I despised my shallowness. Penny had me pegged. I was my father's son.

Belle slapped me side the head again. "Listen here, you dolt. Penny didn't tell you because she knew you'd do exactly what you did. Run off."

"Okay, I get it. I'm a man, ergo I'm an idiot. Now don't hit me again."

"I won't if you wise up."

"What do I do, Belle? I want to run, but I still love her."

Belle leaned back in her chair. "First, end this self-pity party right now. You asked for the truth. Just because you don't like what you hear doesn't mean you need to act like a spoiled brat."

"You don't understand, Belle. R.J.'s been my world since the day he was born."

"Let me ask you this. If Penny had a kid before the two of you met, would that have made a difference?"

"I'd like to think I'm a good enough man I could accept a stepson. It's different where R.J.'s concerned. I'm so proud of him. He loves his old man as much as I love him. A man prides himself on how a son looks up to him like a hero—when he asks you a question you can't answer because he thinks you're the smartest person in the world. Penny took that away from me tonight. How can I forgive her?"

"It takes more than DNA to raise a kid. R.J. looks up to you because he knows you love him. Admiration like his is precious. He's a neat kid. Lots of men would give their right arm to have a son like R.J., their blood or not."

My cheeks heated with self-loathing.

"Could be God knew what would happen and brought you to the Oasis at the right time to help Penny. Maybe you should consider

God's plan a compliment. He knew R.J. would need a father, and he picked you."

Anger welled anew at my lack of substance. "Interesting thought. I'd like to believe I'd have stuck by Penny if she'd told me back then."

"Are you so sure?"

I hung my head in shame. "No. I'm not."

"You can't go back to yesterday, so you'll never know the answer for sure. You can, however, move forward. If you love Penny as much as I think you do, give her a chance to explain why she kept her rape a secret until now. You run out on Penny, you'll desert a boy who loves you. Like your father did. Besides, if her rape happened so soon before you married her, can you be so sure R.J. isn't yours?"

I gulped down the rest of my coffee. I wanted to run to the real bar next door as was my habit when Belle's wisdom struck an uncomfortable chord.

"Now get out of here before I boot you out."

I went back to *The Beast*. I'd thought I was the kind of man who stayed in the game, and I always tried to do whatever expectation was put on me—I remembered the shed—eventually. I was the poster boy for phoniness—my life a Niagara Falls of self-delusion.

Funny how we expect perfection from others; yet we find a gazillion excuses when it comes to our own failures. I considered myself to be a compassionate man. Here I was ready to skip Granite Falls. I'd judged my mother, my wife, and my father for their sins, yet felt justified to commit one of my own.

I drove *The Beast* through more country roads before I made a last definitive swerve and headed back to Maple Street. What waited for me there? Belle's years of mini-sermons scooted through my brain as I tried to make sense of this day. I denied belief in a personal God as much as I denied my unrighteousness.

Whenever I looked into my wife's eyes, I wanted to believe in God because I knew I'd married his special creation. There is a lake not far from Granite Falls where the water is so pure you can see clear to the bottom. How I felt whenever I gazed into Penny's eyes—I saw my exposed soul. Or so I'd thought.

Were these more delusions? Was I a sinner or a victim?

I pulled into the house on Maple Street near midnight, surprised the lights were still on. A gray Toyota Corolla with Tennessee license plates plugged the driveway so I parked on the side of the road. Maybe Millie decided to stay the night.

"Mom, everything all right in here?" I called out as I opened the kitchen door.

I recognized the faded paisley scarf and tarnished gold pin worn by the attractive, middle-aged woman sitting across the table from my mother. Though in a state of flux, I noticed a nativity set now rested where Millie's picture had reigned for all these years.

"Pretty, isn't it," Mom said. "A gift." She turned toward Millie. "This is Ryan."

Millie smiled. "My, he's a handsome boy, Bertie. You must be proud."

Mom wriggled her shoulders. "I am. He's a good son."

At the moment, I didn't feel like a good son. Mom's declaration of a saintliness I knew I lacked only further smashed my pride.

I'd never enjoyed small talk, uncomfortable in social situations; and idle talk with a ghost was not on my immediate agenda. Still, I knew Mom expected me to be civil in spite of my personal worries. I gathered enough courtesy to nod in acknowledgment. "Your visit means a great deal to my mother."

Mom motioned for me to sit.

"Millie, I don't mean to be rude. I need to talk to my wife."

Mom crossed her arms. "Sit, Ryan. Wait a few minutes before you go into Penny's room again. You need to hear what Millie has to say."

"Mom, you don't understand—"

"You're wrong. I do understand. Completely."

"You know what has troubled Penny all this time?"

She nodded. *Aha.* So she was a co-conspirator. "Why didn't you tell me?"

"Not my place, Ryan. Though, since I've been going to church, you and Penny have constantly been in my prayers. When she got the picture in the mail, I managed to get her to talk about it. It's brought us closer. Until then, I don't think we ever truly knew one another."

Millie glanced toward my mother. A familiar aura surrounded Millie—the same kindness I sensed with Belle and Gina. "Go ahead, Bertie. Ryan needs his mother right now."

Mom nodded and motioned for me to sit. "Penny told me what her boss did to her, then I told her about your father. She made me promise not to say a word to you. I encouraged her, on more than one occasion, to be honest with you. No one knows better than me how much it hurts to tell the truth. I have also learned deceit is far more destructive."

Millie glanced in my direction. "Your mother told me you have issues to work out with your wife. I don't want to be in the way. Bertie thought I might be of help."

"Ryan, Millie told me all she went through after she ran away. You need to hear what she has to say."

"Mom—I will—after I see Penny."

"No. On this, please, trust me. Talk with Millie, first."

I met Millie's gaze; compassion beamed from her eyes. I sat. "I'm open for advice if you have any."

"Do you play baseball?"

Strange question. "I'm familiar with the game."

"In life, we all have to take our turn at bat. Some of us, though, only get curve balls. However, striking out is not inevitable. Your mother and I were thrown one hard pitch after another. As I look back, I see God's hand on every pitch."

Mom's eyes misted. "Ryan, listen to Millie."

I shook my head at the irony. Was this how God answered prayer? Let my life fall apart at the same time he puts my mother's back together?

Millie, Gina, and Belle believed in a different God than Grandma Brown's. Maybe God only cared about good-hearted former nuns and repentant runaway teenagers, and the rest of us had to muddle through as best we could.

I glanced toward the den. Should I go to Penny now or heed my mother's advice? The answer came as Mom plopped a cup of hot chocolate in front of me, a hot beverage her panacea for all of life's ills.

MIRACLE ON MAPLE STREET

Millie
December
1961

I ran blindly into the rain to catch up to Stoney and failed to notice the patch of ice ahead of me. I fell, full force on my stomach, unable to breathe for a minute or two. With great effort, I pulled myself to a stand then glanced frantically in every direction. No sign of Stoney. I screamed his name. If he heard me, he chose not to answer. Loneliness chilled more than the icy flakes.

I couldn't go back home. Where else could I go with no money and only the clothes I wore. I shivered. I'd need to find shelter or freeze to death. I followed the road into town. Maybe I could take cover at the bus stop.

Main Street stretched like a barren desert, the only other human in sight was a drunk sprawled on the sidewalk. Was I now destined to live the same life as this derelict? Exhausted, I sat on a bench in front of Heidi's Beauty Parlor—filled with the realization I'd never find Stoney.

Jonas believed in a God of desperate causes. I'd never felt as desperate as now. "I know I don't deserve your help, God, but I have nowhere else to turn."

Sleet turned into heavy flakes of snow. Maybe God didn't hear me. Since I'd broken more than one commandment, I figured he'd turned a deaf ear.

Two spheres of light shone through the white night. Soon, Jonas' truck pulled up in front of me. "Get in," he said.

I obeyed.

"You foolish girl. Why did you run off?"

I blubbered as I rested my head on Jonas' shoulder. "Stoney's gone. I don't think I'll ever see him again. I don't know what to do. Daddy's always had a mean temper, but I've never seen him get so angry he wanted to murder someone. He'd have killed Stoney if I hadn't stopped him."

"We don't know that for sure. Maybe he only meant to scare the lad."

"I disappointed Daddy so much. Will he ever forgive me?"

Jonas handed me his handkerchief. "Your father will come around in time. He loves you. For the moment, he's lost control. I've always been able to talk him through his tempers. This time, might take a while. Before I left, Walter had brought up a case of Seagram from the cellar. Never knew it was there. I don't want you at the house if he's drunk. You shouldn't go back home until I know it's safe."

"Where else can I go?"

"I have a friend in Albany who runs a home for unwed mothers. Let me give her a call. Once I get you settled, I'll go back and deal with Walter. You'll see. Everything will be fine in God's good time."

"Daddy's been sober for ten years. It's my fault he's drinking again."

"No, Millie. You're not responsible for the bad choices other people make."

I leaned back against the seat.

"Stay here in the truck where it's warm while I call my friend. I'll be right back."

Jonas returned in what seemed only seconds. "It's all arranged. My friend, Mrs. Simmons, agreed to give you a place to stay. Most of the girls she takes in are on government assistance. She said she'd be happy to work out a private arrangement as a favor to me."

"How do you know Mrs. Simmons?"

"She's a widow lady who I met at my church a few years back. We were engaged for a short time."

"I never knew you were engaged."

"I was. You were still pretty young, so you probably didn't remember her."

"Why didn't you get married?"

"One day, she said she inherited a big house in Albany. Said the Lord told her to use it to start a ministry for unwed mothers. She calls it Elizabeth House."

"After the mother of John the Baptist?"

"No. After the first girl Mrs. Simmons tried to help."

"Tried?"

"The girl died from a back-alley abortion."

"That's so sad."

"We were called for different purposes, I suppose. She had a mission in Albany. Mine was to stay in Granite Falls. We've kept in touch over the years."

Jonas had sacrificed so much to keep Daddy sober and take care of me. I'd let the both of them down.

Blessed sleep took over for the two-hour ride to Albany.

I woke as Jonas turned into a driveway. I stared at my temporary home, a mammoth Victorian estate. "I don't have any clothes or even a toothbrush. There isn't any place open this late on Christmas Eve."

"Mrs. Simmons often has to take girls in at crazy hours. She keeps an emergency supply for those situations. She'll take good care of you. I trust her."

Jonas had trusted Stoney, too. I had no alternative but to hope Mrs. Simmons was God's answer to Jonas' prayer.

He shoved a twenty-dollar bill in my hand. "It's all the cash I have on me. I'll be back to check up on you in a few days. After the shock of tonight, you need to rest. We'll get through this, I promise."

"What about Stoney?"

"Don't worry about him."

"He doesn't know about the baby."

Jonas glared. "The weasel's probably on his way to New York by now. You're better off without him. I have half a mind to report him to the authorities."

"No, you won't."

"It's called Statutory Rape. You were too young to give consent."

"Stoney never forced me. I won't have my baby's father thrown in jail even if I never see him again."

"Are you sure?"

"Yes. I'm sure. Do I have to give my baby up for adoption?"

"I don't think so. Though maybe you should. If you stay at Elizabeth House any length of time, Mrs. Simmons will help you decide what's best for you. Social workers stop by on a regular basis to counsel the girls."

Rage helped me momentarily transfer blame. "This is all Bertie's fault."

"It's not fair to put all that's happened on that poor girl. Her blurting things out like that didn't help, for sure. But, I'm the one who brought Stoney into the house. Plenty of blame to go around."

I kissed Jonas on the cheek; my second father—in most ways more like a mother. "I'm scared."

"You need to concentrate on yourself. Let me take care of your father. Okay?"

Jonas led me to the door. A pudgy, middle-aged woman greeted us, her hair pulled behind her head in a stubby bun. She gave Jonas a kiss on the cheek then glanced at me. "This must be Millie. You must be frozen what with no coat." She disappeared and quickly returned with an afghan she wrapped around my shoulders.

Jonas scanned as much of the house as he could from his vantage point. "This suits you, Gladys."

"You shouldn't go back to Granite Falls in this storm. You're welcome to stay the night. There's a spare room for guests."

"I'll be fine." He looked out the window. "See? It's already slowed. Besides, I'm used to snow. Remember, I'm from Detroit."

"Be careful, especially through Holcomb. Always snows in Holcomb, no matter what the weather is anywhere else."

Jonas drew me into a fatherly hug. "The sooner I get back to the farm, the sooner I can get your father calmed down. You'll be well cared for here."

I threw my arms around Jonas' neck. "I love you. Tell Daddy I love him, too."

"Deep down in his troubled spirit, he knows."

When Mrs. Simmons closed the door, I summoned courage for the next chapter. Searing pain shot through my back. Was this normal? Did my wanton chase after Stoney hurt my baby? I vowed to be careful from now on, to take care of the life inside of me, to be strong for my child.

Mrs. Simmons led the way to a large parlor filled with girls in various stages of pregnancy. A yuletide log crackled in the fireplace, and a decorated blue spruce took up a larger portion of the room. I sat on an unoccupied chair while Mrs. Simmons introduced me to the girls. The pain worsened with every movement. I longed for sleep. Probably all I needed.

Mrs. Simmons handed me a bag full of toiletries, a nightgown, underwear, and a clean set of clothes. "Normally I require lights out by ten. I make an exception for holidays. We were about to read the Christmas story before lights out." She glanced toward a dark-complexioned girl. "Tessie, here, will be your roommate."

Tessie squealed. "Good. I've been lonely since Lisa went home."

Mrs. Simmons grabbed a big black leather Bible from a mahogany coffee table. "Like you girls, Mary was an unwed mother, though her child had been conceived by the Holy Spirit."

Tessie laughed. "I don't think we got pregnant in the same way as Mary."

Mrs. Simmons smiled as the room filled with laughter. "No. Your pregnancies happened in the usual way between a man and a woman. However, Mary found herself alone and afraid. If angels had not appeared to Joseph as well as Mary, she might have been stoned to death ... what the law at the time required."

One of the girls piped up, "Glad I didn't live back then."

Mrs. Simmons continued. "Mary had no idea how she'd survive, especially if Joseph decided to put her away. The angel told Joseph to take Mary as his wife. They were poor."

Then Mrs. Simmons read from the Bible. I could understand Mary's concern. But how did she trust God to take care of her? I envied that simple faith. I imagined the star over the manger, shepherds visited by angels, and kings who journeyed from afar. Seemed like a very odd way for the Son of the Most High God to come into the world.

"God's ways are not our ways, girls, but you can be certain He will make a way for you. If you repent, give your life over to Him He will forgive you. He will help you through these hard days ahead." She uttered a prayer for each girl to find peace. "Okay, time for bed. Tessie, will you show Millie the ropes?"

Tessie nodded. "Come on. Millie. Follow me."

I quickly realized Tessie was an incessant talker. At any rate, she filled me with all I needed to know about Elizabeth House. "Right now we're on vacation until school starts back up the day after New Year's."

"School? Public school?"

"After we start showing, Mrs. Simmons has a tutor come to the house so we can keep up with our school work."

"Do you know what you'll do after your baby's born."

"I'm due in a week. Mrs. Simmons helps us find foster homes to stay in with our babies if we decide to keep them. Most of the girls opt for adoption. What I plan to do. My baby will have a good home with Mrs. Simmons' pastor. How far along are you?"

"Four months. I only found out for sure a week ago. I was too scared to go to a doctor."

Tessie led me to a room at the end of the hall. "Ours is the farthest away from the bathroom, but it's the biggest. Win some, lose some." She eased herself onto a bed. I assumed the other would be mine. Tessie pointed to a dresser next to my bed. "You can put your belongings there."

She yawned. "I'll probably drift off real quick. So don't think you'll keep me awake. Turn off the light when you're ready to climb into bed." True to her word, Tessie drifted off to sleep almost as soon as her head touched her pillow. Would I ever find peace like that again?

I unpacked the gift bag from Mrs. Simmons then put on the long flannel nightgown, several sizes too big for the moment. I stretched out on a comfortable bed. Too comfortable. I didn't deserve comfort. Nevertheless, sleep—deep and restful—came.

When I woke, yellow sunbeams danced along the carpet. Unusually bright this time of year. I glanced out the window. A fresh carpet of snow sparkled with hope. A sharp radial pain shot across my back. I forced myself to dress then went downstairs.

After breakfast, we were allowed free time to read or write letters. Some girls made phone calls to wish family members a happy holiday. Thanks to Mrs. Simmons, we enjoyed a hearty Christmas dinner and sang carols around the tree. Afterward, we opened the bounty of gifts Mrs. Simmons provided each girl, me included, though I had arrived in the middle of the night. We fell into bed exhausted from a long day of festivities, too busy to drench ourselves in worry.

The next morning, Mrs. Simmons said a social worker would stop by in a day or two to discuss options for my baby. Jonas had promised to be here today as well. Why hadn't he called by now? Maybe it took a lot longer to calm Daddy down than Jonas expected. Tomorrow, Mrs. Simmons planned to shop for maternity clothes as well us sundry personal items I might need. She'd found a few skirts and tops left behind by other girls. None of them fit, but at least they were clean.

Seemed I slept the whole day away between bouts of nausea. When I woke the following morning, a plan began to take shape, and for the first time since I left Cold Creek, I felt hopeful. Jonas' God had heard my pleas. I checked the time—seven o'clock. Still half an hour before breakfast, though I had no appetite. Seemed

I'd been sick the whole of my pregnancy, more so since I arrived at Elizabeth House.

Thankfully, most of the girls had already gone downstairs; only Tessie remained asleep, her tummy like a mountain underneath the covers. I rubbed my stomach to examine the slight bump on my abdomen. How soon before I waddled like the others? A ring of pain shot around my middle like an electric shock.

Dizzy, I slid along the walls to the bathroom, surprised to see Tessie still in bed when I returned. I dressed quietly, but let out a slight, "ouch" when I pricked my finger on the gold leaf pin Bertie had given me. I rubbed the paisley scarf against my cheek as my eyes misted. Would I ever see my friend again? I should call to let her know I was okay. At the least, I'd ask Jonas to make contact on my behalf. Maybe she'd like to visit me, and we could listen to Elvis records. I talked to the scarf. "You'll see, Bertie. Everything will be fine. You were right to tell Daddy."

I jumped at the loud rap. Tessie rolled over with a moan.

"It's Mrs. Simmons. May I come in, dear?"

I buttoned the polka-dotted maternity blouse provided for me. "Of course."

Tessie sat up with a start as Mrs. Simmons came into our room. She rubbed her eyes. "What's going on?" She glanced at the clock. "Oh, dear. I better hurry. Don't want to miss breakfast. Baby's hungry." She lumbered out the door, presumably to the bathroom. I glanced up at Mrs. Simmons who held a copy of *The Albany Herald*.

"Millie, you need to sit."

The movement to the bed brought on another sharp pain, the worst one yet. I kept the discomfort to myself.

Mrs. Simmons sat next to me, her face taut with concern. "Please understand I didn't know about any of this until I read today's paper."

"What happened?"

"There's been an accident. Jonas. Apparently, his truck slid off the bridge in Holcomb."

"Is he all right?"

"No, Millie, he's not."

"He's dead?"

Mrs. Simmons nodded.

I wept for Jonas. How much my father needed him—how much I needed him.

My tears spent, Mrs. Simmons face remained grave. "I called the police to verify. They're on their way over to talk to you. They've been looking for you since Christmas."

Her eyes reflected more bad news to come.

"What do they want with me, Mrs. Simmons?"

"It's about your father."

"Is Daddy okay?"

Mrs. Simmons told me the awful thing Daddy did to himself. She must be mistaken. None of what she said made sense. I wanted to argue, to lash out verbally since I couldn't pound the walls. I opened my mouth to scream; instead, I arched with pulsating pain. The room went black as a gush of warm blood filled my underwear—my last conscious thought—*Daddy!*

🍁

I stirred, aware of a presence near my bed. "Bertie, is that you?"

She giggled. "No it's, Tessie."

"Can't be. Tessie's about to have a baby. You're too skinny to be Tessie."

"She's awake, Mrs. Simmons."

A large-framed woman rose from a chair and stood next to my bed. When my eyes finally focused, I noticed swirl designs on the wallpaper. This was not my room. Where was I?

Mrs. Simmons took my hand. "I'm so glad to see you alert. You scared us, Millie."

I needed to vomit. Mrs. Simons handed me an oval-shaped pink basin. When nausea left, I examined my surroundings once more. "Mrs. Simmons, where am I?"

"You're in the hospital, dear.

"Hospital? Why? What's wrong?"

"You had to have an operation."

Memory can be cruel. "Daddy! Jonas!"

My tears fell like a tropical storm while Mrs. Simmons cradled me in her arms. Grief suspended, I fell asleep within a blanket of comfort.

When I woke again, Mrs. Simmons fussed over a breakfast tray. "You should try to eat. The doctor said you're malnourished. Might explain your sunken eyes."

"Then this isn't a nightmare. I'm in the hospital like you said. Jonas … my father? They're both dead?"

Mrs. Simmons pulled me into a hug as we cried together.

I wiped my eyes. "What about their funerals? Do you know? I should go."

She hesitated before she said, "Millie, you were so sick. Once I knew you were out of danger, I called your Aunt Donna. She hung up on me before I could explain who I was. Then I talked to an editor at the Cold Creek newspaper office. There were no arrangements for your father other than a prayer by the funeral director. Jonas' arrangements were managed in Detroit by his brother."

"Did Aunt Donna ask about me?"

Mrs. Simmons didn't answer.

"I don't want to go back to Cold Creek. I've made up my mind to keep the baby. Jonas said there were social workers who'd help me."

Mrs. Simmons' face paled. Instinct told me the worst news was about to follow. I remembered Mrs. Simmons' earlier explanation as to why I'd been brought to the hospital."

"You said I had an operation. For what? Is the baby okay?"

"The doctor will be in to talk to you. He'll answer all your questions."

I grabbed her hand. "No. I want you to tell me."

She closed her eyes, her cheeks wet. "Oh my poor, dear."

"I lost the baby, didn't I?"

She nodded.

First Jonas. Then Daddy. Now my baby? "That's why I had an operation? I had a miscarriage?"

"More complicated than a miscarriage, I'm afraid. The doctor will explain."

"I don't want to wait for the doctor. Tell me what happened."

She hesitated and stammered a reply, "Your uterus was badly damaged—"

"Did they repair it?"

Her hesitancy told me what I feared.

"I had a hysterectomy?"

She nodded.

Maybe I'd shed all my tears already for Jonas and Daddy. I had none left to give my baby. Where grief should have heaped upon grief, I felt numb. God rightly punished me.

Somehow sleep overtook me. When I woke, Tessie stood next to me.

"Am I still in the hospital?" I asked.

"Uh-huh."

"Then why are you in your nightgown?"

"I'm a patient."

"You had your baby?"

"A girl like I hoped."

"And you still decided to give the baby away?"

"Yep."

"Aren't you sad?"

"No. I made the best decision for both of us. Pastor Lionel said I can visit my baby whenever I want. It's called an open adoption. I got to hold her today. She's beautiful. Pastor Lionel let me pick out a name."

"What?"

"Sarah, after my mother."

"A very pretty name."

Mrs. Simmons came into the room. She squeezed my hand. "How are you feeling?"

"I'm not sure."

"The police are here along with an attorney the court assigned to represent you regarding your father's estate."

She said it as if the court thought my father had money. As far as I knew, I'd have to sell off the property lock, stock, and barrel to cover his debts. There'd be precious left if any. At sixteen, I'd become a pauper and would be completely on my own.

Two uniformed officers came in with a young woman. They all introduced themselves, and the young woman said she was a court-appointed law guardian. I told them what happened at my party. They told me Stoney Rivers was actually somebody named Harry Stockwell, a con artist wanted in several states under additional aliases. I signed paperwork for the attorney. "Do I have to go back to Cold Creek?"

The taller of the two officers shook his head. "You're sixteen. We can only advise and assist. We can't force you."

"I'd rather live on the street than go back to Cold Creek."

The other officer looked at the attorney. "I'm sure you won't have to become a vagrant."

Mrs. Simmons held my hand. "No, you won't."

The law guardian nodded. "We'll help you find a place to live. You won't have to camp out on the street."

When the police left, I trembled at my uncertain future. No money and no means of viable support. "I'm an awful person, Mrs. Simmons. My father, Jonas, my baby. I'm to blame for it all. I deserve whatever punishment God puts on me."

Mrs. Simmons rocked me in her arms. "Oh, my dear, dear girl. You made a grown-up mistake, but your life is far from over. You'll get well. You'll go on to live a productive life. You will find God's perfect plan for you."

"Where will I go?"

"If you agree, I'd like for you to stay on at Elizabeth House. I need help. And I suspect you are a good worker. I'll see to it you're enrolled in school. Smart girl like you should be able to get a scholarship for college. I'll do all I can to help you."

I gulped at the undeserved kindness. "Why would you do so much for me?"

"It's my Christian duty. Besides, Jonas loved you like a daughter. He was very special to me. So you see? You're like a daughter to me, too."

How could I think about tomorrow when all I longed for was yesterday? I wanted to go back in time to when Bertie and I listened to records and watched *Perry Mason*. Only, I couldn't go back. If I were to move forward, I would have to shed this guilt. Easier to throw blame elsewhere.

This is your fault, Bertie. I never want to see you or Cold Creek again.

Millie
September
1966

Three weeks into my senior year at Arlington College, I paced my dormitory room, consumed by a restless spirit. My future was set, wasn't it? I'd begin my student teaching in the spring then next fall I'd start grad school. Why did I feel so uneasy?

I returned to my Old Testament memorization assignment as I recited my favorite from Psalms. *Why are thou cast down, O my soul? And why art thou disquieted in me? Hope thou in God; for I shall yet praise him for the help of his countenance.*

I reminded myself of how good God had been to me over these past years. Yet, this unnamed cloud continued to hover over my soul.

I fondled the paisley scarf Bertie had given me as I slipped the gold leaf pin in place. *Oh, Bertie, I still miss you, so much. I hope you've found a way to be happy.*

When I gave my heart to the Lord, anger fled. Over time, I learned to forgive Bertie as well as Stoney. I wanted to find her, to let her know how well my life turned out. How God had used my troubles to draw me to him. Over the summer, I tried to call Aunt Donna only to discover the line had been disconnected. I wrote Bertie a letter, not surprised when it came back as undeliverable. The dead end a good excuse, I gave up the search. This way I could bury Cold Creek memories further into the pit of forgetfulness. Best to let the past rest.

I headed for a lecture at Sweeney Hall presented by a senior, Lyle Weston. No one I knew. I'd gone to earn extra credit offered by my

Ethics professor. He helped organize the lecture series for promising seminarians to provide a means to test their speaking skills. The extra credit incentive assured the students of a few attendees in addition to reluctant faculty. Coerced and bribed listeners made for a tough audience.

I went with the expectation of complete boredom. None of the lectures so far stirred me to the desired action. When I sat in the back row, Lyle's gaze veered toward me. His rugged demeanor compensated for large ears, a prominent nose, and a crooked smile. On anyone else, those features might be deemed homely. His broad shoulders showed off his athletic build. Magnetic blue eyes drew me in.

The fact we had never met before didn't surprise me. Seminarians followed a different academic path than liberal arts students. I'd chosen a career in education, not because of limited career choices for women. This had been the Lord's direction for me. Faith made the choice, not men's inclination.

My ears perked with the first line to his homily. "Do you walk by faith or by whim?"

This man intrigued me, one who was not afraid to confront traditional religious thought. He finished his speech to a standing ovation. I watched in admiration as faculty crowded him with congratulations. At the least, I wanted to extend my appreciation for his thoughts. "My name is Millie Cooper."

"Yes. I know."

"You know me?"

His smile exuded inner peace.

"Dr. Onifur's church history class. You sit in the front row. I've never heard any girl ask the deep questions you do."

I blushed to think I hadn't noticed him before now.

"I enjoyed your sermon. I like your ideas."

He stuffed his notes into his briefcase. "If you'd like to hear more of them join me for a milkshake at the student union."

Millie
May
1967

Lyle kissed me then picked up his briefcase. "Tonight I want to take you to the Neptune Restaurant."

"It's horribly expensive to eat there. Are you sure?"

He kissed me again. "Absolutely. I want tonight to be memorable."

Lyle planned to attend graduate school at Georgetown, while I'd been accepted at Yale. Would we continue to date? I hoped so. He treated me as an intellectual equal, even when my opinions differed from his.

He kissed me a third time—his desire evident.

I tingled with excitement, yet pushed him away. "Go to class."

He whistled as he left.

Until today's third kiss, our relationship had made no demands on one another. I could not ignore his implicit want for me. Could I give my love to a man after what happened with Stoney? He'd stolen my innocence. If I made love to a man again, would I compare the experience to the first time?

How could I be sure I loved Lyle? I thought I loved Stoney. He deserted me. Lyle's faith would require him to consummate love through the sanctity of marriage. Did he plan to propose? Is this how he intended to make our date memorable?

If we married, he'd want children. I knew I couldn't have any, but had never told Lyle about my operation or anything about my pregnancy. Nor had I told him what happened to Daddy and Jonas.

Lyle deserved a wife as new to love as he. And he'd want children. My heart sank. I'd have to break up with him before our date tonight. How could I let him propose then tell him marriage was not God's plan for me?

I called him, and we agreed to meet in the Quad after his last class. When we embraced, my resolve weakened. I gathered the courage to push him away.

He scowled. "What's wrong?"

I couldn't look at him, or I'd lose all determination. "I don't know where to start?"

He led me to a nearby bench. "Okay, start anywhere. We'll sort through whatever bothers you once it's in the open."

I veered my gaze toward a budding lilac bush. "I sense you want more out of our relationship."

"You sense correctly."

I sighed and nearly choked on my words. "I don't think we should see each other anymore."

"Millie, look at me."

I turned.

"What's really going on here?"

"I don't think we should see each other anymore. Please don't make this so hard. My mind's made up."

"I don't believe this is what you really want. At least have the decency to explain why you don't believe we should be together."

"I don't want to."

"Please. Tell me. I have a right to know."

I knew he'd pester me until he discovered the very truth I fought hard not to tell him. "If I tell you, you will despise me."

"Millie, I love you. I could never despise you."

"You know I'm an orphan—"

"Doesn't matter to me."

I talked for the next thirty minutes and told every gritty, dirty detail—Stoney, my miscarriage, and my father's suicide. He needed to know the kind of woman he thought he loved. "Now do you understand why we can't see each other after this? You need a wife you can respect."

"I do respect you, more than ever. What kind of a Christian would I be if I didn't believe in God's power to make new what the devil tried to destroy?"

"What about children? I can't give you any."

Lyle slipped to his knee then pulled out a diamond ring. "We'll fill our home with foster children who need a special love. I planned on asking you at dinner tonight. But, there's no better time than now. Millie Cooper, will you marry me?"

Millie
December
1999

Life with Lyle Weston proved to be a symphony of challenges. Perhaps the most difficult were our years in Nigeria, not to mention my husband's impulsive need to scale the world's tallest peaks. His zest for life was only outdone by his commitment to the Lord he loved. From the deepest jungle to the inner cities, I followed wherever God decided Lyle should go. Finally, our path brought us to Nashville, where he accepted a position as prison chaplain and a pastorate at an inner-city church.

Life was hectic. Yet, my past would not leave me. I longed to see Bertie again. One day I shared my desire to find her, and how so far all my attempts had met with dead ends.

"Let's try again. Maybe together we'll have better luck."

"Maybe." The years continued to speed by with appointments, commitments, and obligations to Lyle's ministry. There never seemed to be any time for sleuthing nor could we afford to hire a private investigator.

I convinced myself these road blocks were God ordained. I should keep the past in the past. Why unearth memories long buried?

Lyle suggested we take a vacation to Cold Creek. "Someone in New York has to know where Bertie Brown lives now."

"Sounds like a plan," I said.

A few weeks later, he burst into the parsonage as excited as a little league player who'd made a grand-slam home run.

"You seem pretty chipper tonight," I said.

Lyle led me into the living room. "Sit down."

The last time he'd told me to sit he announced our move to Nigeria. "Don't keep me in suspense."

"There's an inmate I want you to see."

"Why?"

"He asked me to ask you to come see him."

Now I was intrigued. "How does he know me?"

"I think he's your cousin Bertie's husband."

🍁

For as many years as Lyle had been a prison chaplain, I'd never shared his ministry with inmates. Confidentiality laws didn't allow him to talk about the prisoners he counseled. For my part, I supported him with hugs, walks, and diversion. His work took its toll on his emotions. When he'd come home the week before excited he might have found Bertie's husband, I could not refuse to visit the inmate he called Ian McDougal.

I squirmed with each *clink* as I progressed through the prison gates until I reached the privileged visitor's room Lyle arranged for my session with Ian McDougal. I felt claustrophobic within the confines of these small dimensions, about four by four, a short table and two chairs in the middle. A mirror decorated one wall for the guards who stood diligently at the door in the event of an emergency. I didn't know what to expect. I prayed for grace and courage.

I gazed into sorrowful eyes. Yet I sensed his peace—a peace only God can give. He cleared his throat then said, "Thank you for coming."

"My husband is convinced you are my cousin Bertie's husband and said you wanted to meet with me. I must tell you I'm skeptical. How does a man from Granite Falls end up in a Nashville prison?"

"It's a long story."

"Then I suggest you start."

"I don't know where to begin."

My patience waned. Had I wasted my time on a foolish inmate? "I didn't believe my husband at first. Bertie is not an uncommon name."

"I didn't realize the connection until your husband asked my wife's name. One question led to another. We were both amazed when we realized beyond a doubt my Bertie was your Bertie."

"I'm here because you asked. Not because I'm convinced you are my cousin Bertie's husband."

He sat back in his chair. "My wife was originally from Cold Creek. I think that was all I really knew about her before we married. We both worked for a kind couple at a resort lodge in Granite Falls. When we moved into our house in the village, Bertie kept a picture of a young girl on our fireplace mantel. Now that I see you, I'm more convinced than ever that girl is you."

"Why?"

"Your eyes aren't sad like they were in the picture. But it's you all right. The girl wore a paisley scarf with a gold leaf pin. The picture was taken by a Christmas tree."

"You remember so much about a picture?"

"That photograph destroyed our marriage."

My heart skipped several beats, and I thought I'd faint. "It was taken on my sixteenth birthday."

"The night you ran away. I didn't know that part for a long while. Bertie would look at the picture and say, 'She was the best friend I ever had.'"

"I felt the same way. Tell me more."

"Our marriage was happy for the most part. We had a son, Ryan. Good boy. He looked up to me. I worked as a telephone lineman. Every time I put on my yellow hard hat, he'd say, 'Go help people, Pop. That's what heroes do.'"

I smiled. Glad Bertie had a son. Yet confused how my picture had interfered with a happy marriage.

"When I'd leave, I'd ask him to take care of his mother for me until I got back. He'd stand proud and tall, so I knew he'd behave."

"I'm glad she found someone to love. What changed?"

"You see, your picture haunted her. Not so much at first. Over the years, she'd stare at it for longer periods of time. On occasion she'd go so deep in thought, I had to shake her back to the present. On the night I left, a Christmas Eve, she was the worst I'd ever seen her. I finally convinced her to share what happened. How someone named Stoney took advantage of you two … how her mother treated her so badly after your father's suicide. Bertie blamed herself for your father's death and for his friend's accident. She also blamed herself when you ran away. She discovered Stoney had been a con artist. She worried about you … if you found a way to take care of your baby. She needed to know if you were okay."

Tears filled my eyes. I understood Bertie's pain, and I filled with regret for my failure to find her before now. "I couldn't forgive myself for Daddy and Jonas' deaths either. Not until I came to know Christ's forgiveness. Are you a Christian, Ian?"

"I am now. Thanks to your husband. I've worried about Bertie for over twenty years. The night she told me about Stoney … how she'd loved him … how she'd been jealous over your pregnancy … how she ratted on you to your father … how you ran away … all the horror afterward … I acted selfishly. I should have put her hurt ahead of my own. I didn't. You see, she let me believe she'd never been with a man before we married and asked me to show her the ways of love. I could have overlooked what she did with Stoney. But, I'm a prideful man. I got all riled up because she lied to me … too stupid to understand why. My worst regret in life."

Not a person alive who couldn't wish to go back in time—to be given the chance to make the better choice. "What happened?"

"I'm ashamed to say I walked out on her and my boy. I hadn't meant to stay away forever. I needed time to cool my thoughts. I was scared of my own anger. After a couple of days, I planned to swallow my pride, go home and ask Bertie to forgive me for ruining her Christmas, to make sure she was okay."

How very human of him. How well I knew, without a spiritual compass, we make futile attempts to right our wrongs only to worsen our already difficult situations. "Why didn't you?"

"Pride got in my way again. I didn't want to go back empty. I thought maybe I could help Bertie overcome her sadness if I found her brother, Verne."

"What happened to her other brother, John?"

"He died in Vietnam. You and Verne were all Bertie had left. She never made peace with her mother, and she died the winter before Bertie got so bad. I think her mother's death was the proverbial straw—a mental one—more than she could handle. I knew I couldn't find you. Then I remembered Bertie said the last she knew Verne lived in Nashville. Before our big fight, I'd promised to ask for a temporary transfer to Nashville with the intent we'd look for him. What did the poet say about our good intentions?"

"They pave the road to hell."

Ian pierced his lips. I saw years of pain on his haggard face. He coughed then apologized. "I'm a very sick man, Millie. I'm up for parole in a few years. But I don't think I'll live long enough to see the day I'm a free man. End-stage lung cancer."

I ached for Ian. "Is that what you did? Go to Nashville? How did you end up incarcerated?"

"I thought if I found Verne, Bertie might be more apt to forgive me. I didn't think I'd be gone long. I got a leave from my boss, found a temporary room in Nashville and played the guitar at a local bar for tips. I asked around. I knew Bertie could sing. Maybe her brother tried to break into country, why he went to Nashville. I finally got a good lead. He'd had a gig at a nightclub not far from where I played. I thought maybe my detective work would pay off."

"It didn't?"

"I discovered he'd died in a brawl a month before."

Why did God allow so much tragedy into one family? Then I remembered life is about the choices we make. After Bertie's father had died, Aunt Donna became a bitter woman in spite of her so-called faith. She'd poisoned her three children against her … and Daddy, too. As for my father, he'd been an alcoholic. He made a choice to drink the night I ran away. The human mind wants to blame God for troubles caused by one bad decision after another.

Faith helped me see this truth. I prayed for Bertie. I prayed for God's mercy on her and her family.

"You didn't go back home after you discovered what happened to Verne?"

"Pride's a terrible sin, Mrs. Weston. I felt like a failure and drowned my woes in a bottle of Jim Beam. I missed Bertie and my boy so much. I got into my truck with intent I'd go back home to Granite Falls, get on my knees, and beg Bertie's forgiveness. I had no business behind the wheel, inebriated as I was. Before I got out of town, I ran a red light and hit a woman crossing the street. She died. Turned out she was the wife of a local politician. The judge was hard on me. I was sentenced to twenty-five years for vehicular manslaughter."

I didn't know how to answer him. I felt bad for Bertie, yet, understood the severity of his crime. Who was I to second guess a judge's decision? The fact he'd never told Bertie seemed more unforgivable than his drunken act.

"I know what you think. You wonder why I never told my wife where I was. At first, I believed Bertie was better off thinking I'd run away for good than to know the man she loved was a murderer. Accidental or not—I deserved my punishment. I hoped Bertie would divorce me and go on with her life. As months turned into years, I never found the courage to write. Until I met your husband."

"Have you written to her?"

"Yes."

"Then why did you want to speak with me?"

"I asked your husband how much you knew about Bertie. If you ever found her. He told me you've suffered, too. I asked the Lord what I should do. I've written Bertie a letter that explains what I did and where I am. I'm not certain if she still lives in Granite Falls. Pastor Lyle said he'd try to find her address if she'd moved."

"Why did you feel it necessary to tell me all this?"

"I hoped you'd take my letter to her. Pastor Lyle agreed you should."

My breath hitched. Year after year, I'd prayed for a miracle to find Bertie. Now, after four decades, God would lead me to her. Why now? What could possibly be gained by a visit with a letter sure to add more misery? What if Bertie had remarried, found a new life? Would my visit and Ian's letter add to her distress? Hadn't she suffered enough?

"Ian, I don't know what to say. I need to think about your request."

"Mrs. Weston, I understand why you might not want to see Bertie. All I ask is that you consider the possibility and pray about it. I'm confident you'll do what's right."

With that, my visit to Ian McDougal ended with no clarity as to what I should do about his request. God certainly did work in mysterious ways—convoluted ways to a finite mind—nonsensical ways to challenge the most devout faith in a merciful God.

When Lyle came home that night, he immediately pulled me to the couch. "How was your visit with Ian?"

"I'm not a carrier pigeon." I felt the venom in my words, and my cheeks heated with shame.

His face drooped. "I thought—"

"I know what you thought. I'm sorry I snapped at you. I don't know what to do, Lyle. I'd like to find her, but what would I say after all this time? Isn't status quo for the best?"

Lyle's scowl squelched my defense. I broke into deep sobs.

"I confirmed with the post office. Bertie still goes by McDougal and lives at the same address in Granite Falls. You need to go see her. I think you've been as haunted these forty years as she has. You both deserve to find peace. If you decide to go, I'll take you."

The only promise Lyle ever failed to keep.

The day he died, Lyle had preached on forgiveness, perhaps the most passionate sermon of his career. In retrospect, perhaps he'd written the sermon solely for my benefit as if he knew he would not be able to keep his promise.

"We're quick to identify fault in others," he'd said, "and huff with pride when we are the first to extend forgiveness. Most often, wrongs are two-sided and equally borne. Until we seek forgiveness for our part, the process is incomplete."

After church, he complained of a headache and laid down to rest. In all our married years, Lyle never took naps. He went to bed and fell into eternal sleep.

At his funeral, I wept. "I promise. I'll find Bertie."

With Christmas on the horizon, I felt compelled not to delay. A few days after Lyle's funeral, I placed my suitcase in the trunk then handed my house keys to the head elder. Though no one pressured me, I knew the church would need the house for a new pastor. I asked for a little time to make a much-needed journey. When I returned, I'd vacate as soon as possible. I needed to find Bertie and deliver Ian's letter as I promised.

Lyle would not want me to mourn him. Least of all use his death as an excuse to avoid a mission. As I pulled onto the highway, fear mingled with determination. "God, plow the fields before me so together we'll reap a harvest."

Ryan
Christmas
1999

The clock struck twelve and Christmas Day came whether we wanted it to or not. Mom handed me Pop's letter. "Read this. Ryan, your father's alive, and he still loves us."

I skimmed the letter then gave it back to her.

My mother's hopeful gaze searched for some response. She had found comfort in my father's words. Not me. My resentment found new levels of animosity. How could Pop have been so stupid to think a few words on a piece of paper made up for his absence? He'd made foolish choices—the first, to walk out on my mother—the second, to get drunk. Then he had the audacity to think we'd offer forgiveness like a plate of Christmas cookies?

When my father disappeared, I clung to various theories through the years. My favorite was the idea he must have been abducted by aliens. I accepted any explanation other than the fact I'd disappointed him. At least, the letter put to rest any notion of blame on my part or my mother's.

Mom placed Pop's letter on the table. "Ryan, will you take me to see him?"

"I'll think about it. Right now, I need to deal with my own marriage problems."

I never thought of my mother as a profound thinker, yet sometimes her philosophies about life amazed me. Once I complained to Penny, "The volleyball net is so loose we should throw it out and buy a new one."

Mom harrumphed into the house, came out with twine, looped it through the net then pulled the ends around the pole. As taut as when it was new. She slapped her hands together. "Sometimes a thing isn't as broken as it seems."

Could my marriage be as simply repaired?

I remembered how I held R.J. the day he was born. I wept as I cried to Penny, "Look what we've made!" Still weak, she smiled. Then my baby boy gripped my finger. I kissed his little cheek. "I'll never leave you, Sonny."

How deeply I'd been deceived. My anger surged again. I looked for something to smash.

Mom squeezed my hand. "The devil loves to fill our heads with blame and guilt. Don't let him win, Ryan." She turned to Millie. "We can't change yesterday. That doesn't mean we have to get mired down in bad memories. The only remedy is to make new ones—good ones—and hold onto those."

Maybe for some, life ends far better than it begins. Detours take us to new destinations—places not found even in our dreams. I thought about the roads Mom and Millie took out of Cold Creek to merge on Maple Street at the same time I faced a decisive intersection in my life. What road should I take?

Mom pushed me toward Penny's room. "It's time, Ryan."

Millie nodded. "You may not fully believe, but God has a plan in all this. The choice is yours. You can accept His solution, or go your own way."

Mom tweaked my cheek. "You're a good man, Ryan. I'm confident you'll do what's best for your family."

There it was, the love I'd craved from my mother since my eighth Christmas. Yet, I could not claim it, my heart still too hardened. "I need fresh air."

I don't remember how long I walked along Maple Street. As I strolled up and down, I marveled at the variety of decorations. Some people trimmed their whole house with carefully arranged lights while others casually plopped bulbs over their hedges. The house at the end of the block sported a gigantic snowman. I'd always found excuses not to put up outdoor decorations of any kind and left the tree to the women. Ours was the only house on Maple Street with no exterior sign of Christmas.

My soul felt as barren as our front yard. The time had come to give prayer a chance—real prayer—instead of complaints and demands. I asked God to be the mirror into my heart.

I didn't like what I saw. I alone was responsible for my choices. As Lyle Weston preached the day he died—I must admit to my own guilt where my broken marriage was concerned.

Belle Thompson once preached, "God hovers near, ready to forgive, to heal our damaged lives. First, though, we need to know we need Him."

I gazed skyward. If God indeed created the vastness of the universe, couldn't he have protected Mom and Millie from Stoney's depravity? Couldn't he have prevented Uncle Walter's suicide as well as Jonas' accident? Why then didn't he keep Penny from being raped? If God created the universe in six days, he could have kept my father from involvement in a fatal accident, even if he was drunk. Or he could have softened the heart of the judge who sentenced him. How could I worship a God who allowed so much tragedy?

I cringed at my arrogance. Millie believed God worked in our lives regardless of our awareness of him. Gina Forbes said God created mankind with the freedom to make decisions apart from His perfect will. They both believed God was not to blame for the messes we make.

I knelt before Gina Forbes' nativity scene to study the babe in the manger.

God's biggest miracle came in the most vulnerable way—like R.J. I thought how all the grownups in his world had messed up and had been messed up by parents who'd messed up, generations upon generations of messed up folks unwilling to accept God's redemption. Seemed I had a choice to make. I could try to do what I thought was best for me based on my own skewed concept of morality. To his condemnation, my father thought he could fix his mistakes on his own. Or, I could turn the whole mess of my life over to God.

Easier thought than done.

Tears froze on my cheeks as I looked toward R.J.'s bedroom and resumed my prayer. "I'm sorry for my sins of arrogance, selfishness, and resentment. Live in me. I can't get beyond this hurt and do what's right for R.J. without you."

I sang *Silent Night* as if for the first time. Today's revelations had brought violent storms into my mundane life. My soul had capsized, and I'd been left adrift. As I heard the words in my heart, calm descended, more renewing than R.J.s bedtime readings. For the first time since childhood, all was calm … all was bright.

I came back into the house through the front door then went upstairs to R.J.'s room, amazed at his innocent sleep underneath the Star Wars comforter Penny had bought for him. Moonbeams cast shadows on his posters. My favorite had always been Luke in a heated battle with Darth Vader. As a boy, I thought maybe the dark side of the force had seduced my father as it had Anakin Skywalker.

Perhaps in some way, it had. Without faith, he lacked the power to overcome his mistakes.

R.J. moaned in his sleep. A nightmare?

No one chased away the monsters underneath my bed. Stone Woman had become too absorbed in her grief, while my hero in the yellow hard hat was nowhere to be found. If I left Penny, who would look for ghosts in R.J.'s closet? A child should never wake up from a bad dream with no one to rock him back to sleep.

I picked up the picture of my mother, Penny, and me that R.J. kept on his nightstand. "So I'll always remember somebody loves me," he'd said.

How could I leave a boy as wonderful as R.J.?

A holy presence, one I'd found only minutes before, surrounded me as I went to Penny's room. When I turned on the light, she raised her head, her eyes, red and swollen, large with surprise. Did she think I'd left her for good?

"What time is it, Ryan?"

"It's Christmas morning."

"You're still here."

"Yes. I'm here."

"I was afraid you'd left us, and I wouldn't have the chance to explain."

"I'm here now. Tell me. Help me understand."

"I don't want to remember."

"You have to. For me. For R.J. For yourself."

"I'm afraid you'll leave again."

"I'm here now. I won't go anywhere until I know what happened." If I'd gained any insight from Mom's revelations, I finally understood how destructive a secret could be. "No more secrets, Penny."

"I don't know if I can remember. I forced the memory from my mind. Then when I got the picture—"

"It all came back?"

"Not everything."

"Who hurt you, Penny? Mom said it was your boss, Gavin."

She nodded. "I don't remember much other than it rained for hours before."

Lord, help me to help her. "We'll put your fragmented memory together piece by piece. Let's start from a time before you knew Gavin."

Penny
Summer
1990

I bowed to accept the applause, then headed backstage and held my trophy high in the air. The win of a local talent contest meant much more to me than the accompanying cash prize. I'd never won anything before in my life. If stodgy Aunt Daisy didn't approve, I knew my parents clapped as they watched from heaven.

I took the rear steps from the platform as a goateed, middle-aged man with shoulder-length blonde hair approached—a man most people in Georgia had forgotten. Not me. I still owned every one of his records. "My name is Declan Harwood," he said and offered a handshake.

"Yes. I know who you are."

He smiled. "Congratulations. You deserved to win. You're very talented." High praise from a once notable country star. "Have you ever considered a career in music?"

Was he serious? *Of course—all I'd ever dreamed about.* "I guess so. It's a big step from a small county contest. Why do you ask?"

He glanced toward the tall, red-headed woman next to him. "This is my wife, Natalie."

She shook my hand as well. "Declan has put together a new band. He hopes to make a comeback. The group needs a female vocalist to round out the sound."

"What about you, Natalie?"

"Me? Honey, I can't even lip sync let alone carry a tune. Declan's made me his manager. We think your voice will fit in nicely."

He took out his business card. "We don't have a name yet. We've considered Country Blends."

"I doubt my guardian would allow me to join a band. She thinks I should only sing for the Lord."

Declan smiled. "I'm a fan of the Big Guy, myself, especially once I got into AA. Ever stop to think maybe church isn't the only place a song can reach a soul?"

"Can I have a day or two to think this over, Mr. Harwood?"

"Call me Declan. Look, as far as your school is concerned, Natalie and I have six kids of our own, the oldest about your age. I'd have one hissy fit if any of them thought they could drop out of school. You can reassure your aunt you'll get your education. I won't abide any dummies in my band, and I don't allow the group to drink on the job. You'd have three burly men to protect you."

Natalie laughed. "Don't forget me."

"I'm sure your aunt only wants what's best for you. I hope she'll realize what a great opportunity we've offered you."

"If she doesn't, I do."

🍁

Aunt Daisy stomped her feet as she shook her cane. "No grandniece of mine will sing in the devil's warehouse."

"Declan said he only accepts invites from respectable establishments."

"God didn't give you a great voice to waste on folks too drunk to listen. I promised your father's lawyer I'd take you in—and I was happy to do so. This is the appreciation I get? If you accept this stranger's offer, I'll disinherit you."

I crossed my arms like a petulant two-year-old. "I don't want your money. I'm sixteen. I can take care of myself."

"Then go pack your bags. I'm done with you … you ungrateful child."

I ran upstairs to use the extension. I could hear Aunt Daisy's raspy breaths on the downstairs line. "I'd love to join your band, Declan. One problem, though. I have to find another place to live. My aunt threw me out."

Aunt Daisy grunted. "Her choice." She hung up.

"Don't worry, Penny. Our house is a little crowded, but we'll make room for you."

Penny
1992

    I'd lived with Aunt Daisy for three years after my parents died in a car accident. We'd gone out for ice cream after church. I dropped my cone in my lap. When I screamed, my father hit a tree. I was told my parents died instantly. I spent a month in the hospital, guilt my constant companion. Why should I survive and they didn't? The only relative I had was Great Aunt Daisy.

    Living with her hadn't been all bad. I had nice clothes, and we traveled a lot. If only she weren't so strict. She wouldn't allow television in the house, and she insisted I go to church every time the doors opened. I knew the arrangement would only be until I went to college. I figured I could tough it out until then. Declan's offer changed everything. How could I pass up an opportunity like this?

    Natalie and Declan became like the parents I'd lost. In some ways, they were even stricter than Aunt Daisy. With so many kids, the house was bedlam. Declan used to say, "I see all the monkeys are out of their cages." My days were filled with as much unpredictability as there was routine. After Declan picked me up from school, we'd go to Chris Tooley's house for rehearsals. Declan made sure he brought me home for supper. When we all sat down to the table, I felt the love of family. Something I'd lost when my parents died.

    Until I met you, those were the best days of my life; I loved the life music gave me. Declan and I carried most of the vocals while the rest filled in with harmony. Our repertoire consisted of country, rock, easy-listening, and oldies. The men wore black leather pants, sequined shirts, and cowboy hats. Natalie thought I should wear a white-fringed cowgirl outfit.

I plowed through two more years of school. After graduation, I waved my diploma in Declan's face. "Top ten of my class. I've proven I'm no dummy, so you can't fire me now!"

He laughed. "We're all very proud of you. Natalie and I planned a party at the house for both you and our daughter. I have a surprise announcement to make. Might call it a triple celebration."

Rows of cars lined up in Declan's driveway and in his front yard. Chris started the barbecue while Natalie set out a picnic supper. After everyone had filled their plates, Declan held his glass of root beer to signal a toast. "Chris, what's the best nightclub in Atlanta?"

Chris grinned. "Without a doubt, the Oasis."

Lane rose. "Natalie?"

"The band starts next weekend."

I couldn't believe our good fortune. Mostly, I was happy for Declan. The Oasis launched the biggest names in country, a grand stage for Declan's comeback.

The next day, we met at the Oasis to sign our contracts. Declan and Natalie talked privately with the owners then returned to the table where the rest of us anxiously waited for the confirmation. "We'll each earn five hundred per performance to start. If we bring in the crowds as Gavin hopes, he'll sign us on as regulars and increase our pay."

Chris took a sip of coffee. "Sounds too good to be true."

I'd never been in the Oasis before, though the place had a reputation second to none. "Is this place haunted, like the rumors say?"

Declan laughed. "Of course not, but it does have a fascinating history."

Chris leaned back in his chair. "Go ahead, professor, fill us in."

"What we now call the Oasis started out as a saloon, Whiskey Haven, built by a carpetbagger named Scarface Hooligan."

I laughed. "You're kidding, right?"

"No. I'm dead serious."

"It's always been a place soldiers gravitate to. Most of Hooligan's clientele were out of work confederate soldiers. Rumor was Hooligan bought up a bunch of plantations and grew barley instead of cotton to supply his distilleries. He ran his business into the ground. Whiskey Haven, along with a number of his taverns, fell into disuse.

"During the prohibition, Tommy Nine-fingers bought the place. He turned it into a speakeasy, but he was killed during an FBI raid."

Lane shook his head and clicked disbelief. "Then what happened?"

"Tommy's son went legit when he inherited the place. At first, he ran it as a restaurant. He bought out the adjoining properties then expanded and called the place The Starlight Lounge. He hired girls to dance with the soldiers. World War II brought him a fortune.

"The place stayed in the family until bought by a music mogul who turned it into the venue it is today. He changed the name to the Oasis and filled it with soldiers. He hired only the best bands as an opportunity for them to be noticed. If any of them signed a record label, he took a percent of the action."

"How did Gavin come by it?" I asked.

"Gavin's brother, Nigel won it in a poker game. Already a multimillionaire with connections in the entertainment industry, Nigel overhauled the Oasis into the premier club it is today. Gavin took over the place when Nigel died."

"Is it true Nigel was murdered?" Lane asked.

"Never was proven one way or the other. His death was called suspicious, since he was found fully clothed, face down in the Chattahoochee River. Some bimbo testified she and Nigel had been out for a walk when he tumbled into the water. No autopsy was done. Some think Gavin killed Nigel, dumped his body in the river and paid for the bimbo's testimony."

Lane rocked in his chair. "Gavin's a snake in the grass all right, though he runs a decent place. We don't have to be friends with the guy. I suppose his personal life is none of our business."

In spite of a reptile for a boss, the gig held great promise. "So what else do we do besides entertain?"

Declan winked. "Make the soldiers happy. A bunch of them come in from Fort Benning. They're the club's lifeline. Gavin thinks a pretty girl like you will be popular with the crowd."

We signed the contracts then celebrated with a round of sparkling grape juice. As we headed out the door, I caught a glimpse of Gavin, decked out in a green Armani suit as he slinked toward the bar, his eyes fixed on me.

🍁

Country Blends packed the house every night, our days busy with rehearsals. In our spare time, we cut a few records, mostly for demo purposes. I soaked in the busyness like a gambler's rush. I looked forward to every weekend.

I didn't mind mingling with the patrons as our contract specified. Sometimes Declan would discover juicy tidbits about a soldier in the audience. After he hauled the victim up on stage, he poked fun at the military. The audience loved the banter. Once Declan found a young man who changed jobs, then we sang "Take This Job and Shove It." Audience participation soon became our trademark.

I finally earned enough to rent my own place. Declan's kids were older now, and he needed all the space he could get in his tiny house. He had supported me long enough. The gig at the Oasis would have been perfect if not for Gavin. I cringed any time he came near me. He always made a point to sit with the band when we took breaks.

I complained to Declan, but he told me not to worry. "Gavin gawks at you because you're pretty. Think of his stares as compliments."

Seemed Gavin lurked wherever I was. I'd never been with boys much at all. Since Aunt Daisy didn't allow me to date, I only had one boyfriend—Jordan—who went to my church. He never tried to get me to do things some of my girlfriends did with their boyfriends. I guess you could say I was naïve about men, and I didn't know how I should handle Gavin.

Declan said the best action was no action. "Ignore him. We keep a close watch on you. If he makes you uncomfortable, don't be alone with him. If he gets fresh with you, let one of us know. I don't expect you to sacrifice your dignity for a gig."

I followed Declan's advice. The more Gavin leered, the more I found him to be a joke, a sad figure of immense insecurity. I no longer feared him.

On any given night, more than one soldier asked me out. I simply said, "Gavin doesn't want band members to date customers." In actuality, the rule was Declan's. Seemed less harsh if I put the let down on Gavin.

I remembered what Declan said—how church wasn't the only place music could touch a soul. Some of the soldiers had sad stories to tell. We closed every performance with "Amazing Grace." Most times, our audience joined in.

Sometimes, I'd think about how proud my parents would have been. Once Declan tapped me on the shoulder. "You look like your miles away, girl."

"I miss my parents."

"You need to find yourself a good man."

"I'm too young."

"Nonsense. I married Natalie when we were both nineteen. We're about to celebrate our thirtieth. She's been the biggest blessing in my life—stood by me through the drunk years. Now, I thank the Lord every day for her. I hope to spend the rest of my life making up for what I put her through before I got sober."

If I could find a man as good as Declan, I'd snatch him right up.

Penny
September
1992

I glanced at my watch. Why was Declan so late? I paced the Oasis then used the time to scour the audience, amused that at eighteen, I was younger than most of the soldiers. Yet, I felt much older. Maybe because I made so much money.

I even asked Gavin if he'd heard from Declan. "Not a word," he said. "With or without him, I expect your band to start on time."

"I'll wait outside for him," I said. I glanced up and down the alleyway where Declan usually parked. No sign of him or his van. Nothing but a few hungry rats. Declan claimed he parked his van in the alley to keep it away from graffiti artists while we performed. I knew the real reason was to make a quick getaway from the lonely housewives' club who shamelessly flirted with him. Declan was a one-woman man.

The last couple of days had seen intermittent rain squalls, with above average temps. Sometimes the rain came down nearly sideways, with heavy gusts. I glanced at the night sky, penetrated by only one dimly lit post near the dumpster. Even in the semi-blackness, the clouds seemed green as they poked near the ground like fingers. A funnel cloud descended from nowhere and spun like a dancing gypsy behind the dumpster. I ran to the door. When I opened it, Gavin stood there, an evil sneer etched on his face. He threw me to the pavement then slammed me against the dumpster, debris flying in circles above me. Before I could get back up, he'd climbed on top of me. I bit, clawed, and kicked with all my strength, but he still overpowered me. I heard my mother's voice, "It will all be over soon."

It was, I think. I had no sense of time, a feeling as if I observed from another plane, detached and unemotional. When done, he grunted then choked me, and I felt life seeping from me. Was this what death felt like?

He let go and slapped my face as I gasped for breath, the funnel cloud dissipating as debris fell to the pavement behind the dumpster. "If Declan even suspects what happened, I'll kill you both." He left me a paralyzed heap of shame. Blood streaked my arm where I'd hit the dumpster. I wanted to run, to leave Atlanta forever. I would have if Declan's van hadn't pulled up.

He rushed toward me as I rose to a stand. "What happened? You okay? What did you do to your arm?"

I remembered Gavin's threat, knew he'd make good on it if I even hinted to Declan about what Gavin had done. "I came out here to look for you and slipped on the wet pavement. Must have hit the dumpster when I fell."

"Are you okay to perform?"

I had to say yes. If Declan sensed I was hurt, he'd force the truth out of me. He'd kill Gavin if he didn't kill Declan first. No need for any bloodshed. "My skirt's a little stained. Otherwise, I'm fine. Start without me. I'll join you after I wash up."

"You shouldn't have come out here. Didn't you get my message?"

"What message?"

"I called Gavin to tell him I had a flat tire and wouldn't get to the club until the last minute. I suggested you canvass the audience while the boys warmed up."

"I haven't seen Gavin yet tonight." I had to vomit but couldn't tell Declan. "Let me freshen up."

I threw up until I spewed only bile then rinsed my mouth with soap to hide the odor. I managed to get the worst of the blood and dirt off my clothes and arm. When I came to the stage, I forced a smile.

In spite of a headache, I sang my heart out. I refused to let Gavin see me as a victim.

On our break, he hovered at our table then called a waiter over to take a group picture. Declan's life depended on my continued calm. Maybe I hadn't done a good job of it since he repeatedly asked me if I was okay.

Gavin put his arm around my shoulder then removed it when Declan frowned. "Your band is one of the best we've had in a long time. I've arranged for an agent to visit next month. And, I've decided to give you all a raise effective tonight."

Acid rushed to my throat.

Chris and Lane gave each other a high-five. Declan glared at Gavin. "Kind of sudden there, Gavin."

"Not at all." He turned toward me. "I should have shown my appreciation a long time ago."

Declan glanced at his watch. "We need to go up for the next set. Penny, you're white as a sheet. Are you sure you're okay? Maybe you should have your arm checked out in the emergency room."

I wiggled my arm as proof. "I'm fine."

As long as I could sing, I believed I'd eventually be okay. After the third set, Declan insisted I go home. I didn't argue, nor did I want to lead the audience in "Amazing Grace." Where was God when Gavin raped me?

When I got home, I stayed in the shower until there was no more hot water. Then I fell into bed. "Close your eyes, Penny. Soon it'll be another day. Everything looks better in the light." I willed the scene from my mind. To keep it buried, I needed to place blame somewhere. I put it on God. Through all my years of Sunday school, "Jesus Loves Me" had been my favorite chorus. A lie. God didn't care about me. I took another long shower in cold water until I was numb from head to toe. I'd take as many showers as needed until I buried my shame beyond any possibility of remembrance. My life—Declan's life—depended on a complete memory wipe.

I begged off rehearsals for the next week—my excuse—my arm was too sore. Declan seemed to understand. I couldn't remember how I'd hurt it in the first place. By Friday, the swelling had gone down, so I reported as usual. For some reason, I couldn't breathe when I came into the club.

I sat for a few minutes, determined not to let a panic attack keep me from my responsibility to the band. The soldiers looked forward to a good performance. When my palpitations lessened, I joined the group on stage. The club seemed inexplicably smaller, every flaw accentuated by things I hadn't really noticed before.

I scanned the sea of soldiers. I could spot them even when not in uniform. One soldier stood out from the crowd, a lanky kid with dark hair who sat close to the stage. You. Your sad eyes said you'd seen a lot of pain in your short lifetime. You clapped enthusiastically and scorned your buddies when they tried to whistle.

When Declan asked if anyone in the audience had a birthday, your buddies raised your arm. Declan especially liked to pick on resistive audience members, so had your friends drag you to the stage. "Where are you from?" he said, and I knew you were in for a whole lot of teasing from a master.

But, you stood tall; your military bearing adding to your charm. "Fort Benning."

Applause erupted.

"Rank?"

"E-four, sir."

"Name?"

"Ryan McDougal, sir."

"Well, McDougal, you can drop the sir. I'm not a drill sergeant."

More laughter.

I admired your spunk. Your wit, so much like my father's, intrigued me.

"How old are you McDougal?"

"Twenty-two today, sir."

"Do you have a request?"

"I'd like to hear 'Good Vibrations.'"

"As long as you sing with us."

You blushed as you joined our rendition. Surprisingly, you possessed a nice baritone.

As you returned to your seat, the audience sang "Happy Birthday."

After the second set, we joined you at your table. I thanked you for your patience with Declan's insensitivity. I leaned forward, rested my elbows on the table, and stared you down until you laughed—a beautiful, sincere laugh. I never flirted for any length of time with an audience member. Yet, you pulled me in. From your accent, I knew you weren't a southern boy nor did you hail from the heartland. So, I asked. "Where're you from?"

"Northern New York. You should go there sometime, especially in the fall when the leaves turn. There's a reason they call the area God's Country."

"Sounds like a great place to live. Girlfriend?"

"No, ma'am." You met my gaze. "Do you want the job?"

I lost myself in your eyes and jumped when Declan tapped me on the shoulder. "Didn't mean to startle you. It's time for our next set."

As I stood to leave, you gave me a look that meant you were going to ask me for a date. I not only encouraged you, I gave you an open door. "I hope you'll stick around awhile longer."

When you asked me for coffee, to Declan's surprise and chagrin, I agreed.

Like the man I've come to know, you stuck around, right through the last session, though you seemed to struggle with the words to "Amazing Grace." For some reason, so did I. Declan scowled, as if confused, since the hymn used to be my favorite part of our act.

I wasn't surprised when Declan tagged along. Always protective. We met you and your buddies at the all-night diner next door. Before long, Declan winked, then left as if he sensed you would keep me safe. "Ryan, will you make sure our lead singer gets home safe and sound?" he asked, with a wink.

You nodded. I think I knew right then and there, we'd end up together.

Soon after, one of your buddies whispered in your ear. They left, and I didn't mind being alone with you one bit.

My short legs made it difficult to climb into your truck. "Where did you find this beast?" I asked.

You laughed. "I bought it off a farmer who said his mutt rode with him wherever he went. Looks like she has a new name. Gonna call her "The Beast," in honor of you."

"Is that a hint I look like a dog?"

You blushed. "No, ma'am. I think you're the prettiest girl I've ever seen."

From any other soldier, the comment would have seemed too forward. Your country blush told me I could trust you.

You stayed the night and shared my bed, but didn't ask for sex. Maybe you sensed I wasn't ready. I didn't know it was possible to fall in love in the space of a few hours.

As if you knew something good was happening, you called your CO to request an extended leave. We spent the next five days together. We kissed a little; you never pushed for more. Although, I think I would have said yes if you had.

I wasn't the least surprised when you suggested we get married. I agreed ... no reason to wait. I felt as right about us as you claimed to feel. We piled into the truck and got hitched in Alabama.

The question of my career never came up, as if we both knew my days at the Oasis were over.

🍁

As soon as we returned from Alabama, you moved us into base housing. As you carried me over the threshold, I giggled like a preteen girl who kisses a boy for the first time. "We're crazy, you know."

You set me down. "Not at all. This is the smartest thing I've ever done in my life." Our hurried marriage brought immediate change. The next few days were hectic with plans to move and begin our lives together. I hated to tell Declan I'd quit the band. I glanced at the plain, gold ring on my finger. Life with you meant far more to me than a platinum record. Each time we nestled in bed, I knew I'd found my soulmate until death parted us.

Ryan
Christmas
1999

I held my wife's hand and wiped away my falling tears. She loved me then and loved me now.

"Ryan, don't you see? I couldn't tell you about Gavin because by the time we met, in my mind, the rape never happened."

I'd spent most of my service stateside. But some of my buddies who served in Desert Storm didn't come back the same. Some refused to talk about what happened over there. Some, however, acted as if they'd never left Fort Benning. A near amnesia of their tour. Sometimes the shock of recall pushed them over the edge. A lot of those guys committed suicide.

Maybe that's how it had been with Penny. I prayed her recall would bring her peace, not more despair. I often wondered why she'd quit the band. Now I understood.

"Do you miss the stage?"

She met my gaze. "Absolutely not. You and R.J. have given me far more joy than I ever thought possible. I'm content with my audience of two."

"But?"

"What now? How do we get past this? That is if it's possible."

I pulled her into an embrace. "I don't know how we'll get past it. I know I want to. We have to, and we will. I don't want to lose R.J. or you either."

"You were so angry when you left. I thought I might never see you again. What made you come back?"

"Had a talk with Belle Thompson ... and Millie who's downstairs with Mom."

"And they helped you?"

"Mostly, I had a talk with the Lord."

"My heart remembers a time when a talk with the Lord solved everything. Before Gavin."

She smiled, lips wet with tears. We'd eventually get past the hurt ... past the shock of revelation—one day at a time, with God's grace.

"What brought it all back?"

"When I got the picture in the email from Chris Tooley. Mostly, disjointed flashbacks. I tried to forget again. Nothing helped. The memories froze like a stuck videotape. I left your bed because of the nightmares. I was too afraid to tell you. You're so proud of R.J. What if it turned out he's Gavin's? I didn't want him to be R.J.'s father. I wanted it to be you. I convinced myself R.J. was too much like you to be anyone else's child. I thought maybe I'd send away DNA samples to find out for sure. If it turned out R.J. was yours, I would never have to tell you about Gavin. Your mother said you deserved to decide for yourself if you should have a paternity test done. I looked for any excuse not to tell you. Then you found the picture—the one I thought I'd destroyed. Maybe your accidental discovery was God's intervention? Maybe he knew I couldn't heal, and we couldn't mend until this awful thing came out in the open."

"I am so sorry you went through something like that. I can't undo it but know this. I love you, Penny McDougall. Nothing will change that ... ever."

We embraced. "You mentioned a letter. Where is it?"

"I hid it on the top shelf of the closet."

"May I see it?"

"Why? I should rip it up. I don't even know why I kept it."

"Please."

She trembled as she reached into a box shoved far behind a pile of blankets, then handed a crumpled paper to me. "Here."

As I read, the bed shook from Penny's shivers.

Hi, Penny!

I expect you're surprised to hear from me. I got your address from Ryan's old CO.

Would you believe I'm getting married? A confirmed bachelor like me? It'd be neat if you were there.

Funny thing happened when I went shopping for a ring. I saw an old van parked outside a restaurant next to the jewelry store. It reminded me of Declan's van. I went to take a closer look, and guess who walked out of the restaurant?

Yep. Declan. We had a long chat over coffee. We talked about the good old days at the Oasis. The band broke up shortly after you left. Lane moved out west. Declan teaches guitar and writes songs. Guess who got sent up on a murder rap? Seems Gavin's bimbo finally decided to confess she'd been paid by Gavin to make the story up. He got life. I say good riddance. Never did trust the guy. As for me? I found another group to drum with. Not as classy as Country Blends, but we've cut a few records. Nothing big yet. Declan showed me this picture of all of us at the Oasis. We got copies made, and he asked me to send you one. I hope you and your soldier are happy. Write when you get a chance.

Love,

Chris

A strange comfort to know Gavin Blackwell would never hurt another innocent. Funny how justice eventually comes full circle. I gave the letter back to Penny. "You should write back, and you should go to the wedding. I'll go with you if you'd like. If Chris had known what Gavin did do you, he never would have sent the letter. He meant well."

Penny put the letter in her dresser. "I don't know. Maybe. If you go with me."

For the second time within the last few hours, I prayed for wisdom. Lyle Weston knew—one person alone cannot cause a relationship to sour. I'd helped the rift grow bigger.

I marveled how God brought a trident of pain together to cause healing. I supposed not all miracles come about spontaneously. Some, I guessed, evolve over months, or even decades. If not for the events of this Christmas, we might never have found our way back to each other. We can't live our lives on what other people should have done or did not do. Still, I wished I'd had more faith in my wife—in us. I ignored her pain, too self-absorbed to see beyond my rejection to her trauma.

"Oh, Ryan. Can you forgive me?"

Forgive her because some jerk assaulted her, and to survive, she wiped the memory from her mind? She was no guiltier for what happened to her than Mom or Millie for what Stoney did to them. I was the one in need of forgiveness.

I kissed my wife and echoed Mom's self-blame. "I'm the sinner in this story."

"What about R.J.? Do you want to take a paternity test or check DNA or whatever it is they do these days? It's possible he's yours and not Gavin's."

"Doesn't matter. A father is more than a bunch of chromosomes. Besides, he takes after me in most ways."

We snuggled in the dark. I could never take away the pain Gavin caused. Thankfully, I'd just met a God who could.

While Penny slept, I spent those pre-dawn hours in prayer, only mildly distracted when I heard the guest room door close. Millie must have decided to stay after all. I was glad she'd spend Christmas with us—glad for the miracles her visit brought—glad for an end to the mysteries that shrouded our home on Maple Street. Glad for the chance to start fresh with new understanding.

Would I make the trip to see my father?

Perhaps someday.

Another story—another miracle.

THE END

About the Author

Award winning author, LINDA WOOD RONDEAU, believes God is able to turn our worst past into our best future, the purpose for her many contemporary novels. Walk with her unforgettable characters as they journey paths much like our own. After a long career in human services, Linda moved from her home near the Adirondack Mountains to Jacksonville, Florida. When not writing, she enjoys playing golf with her husband and best friend in life, Steve. Find Linda on Facebook, Twitter, Goodreads, and Google Plus or visit her website at www.lindarondeau.com.

Made in the USA
Charleston, SC
19 November 2016